Albert Whitcomb Snyder

The Chief Things

Albert Whitcomb Snyder

The Chief Things

ISBN/EAN: 9783337426255

Printed in Europe, USA, Canada, Australia, Japan

Cover: Foto ©Andreas Hilbeck / pixelio.de

More available books at **www.hansebooks.com**

The Chief Things

BY THE

REV A. W. SNYDER.

AUTHOR OF " CHIEF DAYS," ETC.

SECOND SERIES

2 AND 3 BIBLE HOUSE

To that Important but Much-forgotten Creature
"THE AVERAGE MAN"
I DEDICATE THIS LITTLE BOOK

CONTENTS

(5)

Preface.

THIS little book is respectfully dedicated to
"The Average Man." He reads the news-
papers and little else save works of fiction. Ordinarily he will not look at a theological book.
Nor is it very strange. It does not generally
appeal to him. It may be thoughtful and scholarly, but it is too bulky, and not always easily
understood. It demands not a little time and
patience. The "average man" has neither—to
spare. If not scholarly, he is intelligent and
thoughtful. He often thinks of the great questions of faith, duty and destiny, and will gladly
hear them discussed, but it must be with becom-
ing brevity, and in a language that he can understand. He has no time to waste, and so
above all likes lucidity.

It is to this often forgotten man that the author makes his appeal for faith. He believes in
what he says, and has tried to state what he has
to say in a plain straightforward way—"in the
language of to-day, to the men of to-day, for the
needs of to-day."

In this he hopes he has not wholly failed. He will be more than glad should he help any one to Christian believing and living.

A. W. SNYDER.

New York, Trinity Time, 1899.

I.

THE NECESSITY OF BELIEF.

ROMANS xiv. 12.

I.

THE NECESSITY OF BELIEF.

PEOPLE are often roughly classed as believers and unbelievers, but it is an inaccurate, misleading classification. All men believe something. Every man has a belief of some sort unless he is an infant or an idiot. Every human being arrived at years of discretion, thinks. Every man thinks, has thoughts, convictions, opinions; and these constitute his beliefs. All men have their beliefs, such as they are; and their beliefs are to them, at least, of great importance. This will be granted readily enough, no doubt, as regards ordinary affairs, but possibly not so readily as regards religion. It must be seen, however, that the necessity of believing cannot be confined to the affairs of this life only. Not only must every man think, but he must have thoughts of some sort as to religion; must believe of God "That He is, and that He is the rewarder of them that diligently seek Him;" or that there is no God; or that if there be we can have no certain knowledge as to who He is, or as to His will and desire concerning us, or whether He has any. A man's thoughts may not be very clear or definite, still every man has,

11

or has had, thoughts as to these great questions, and they have had a great deal to do with shaping his character, and, therefore, his conduct. Thought and feeling are universal characteristics of human kind. Being involves believing. It is a necessary condition of human existence. A man must think, and because he thinks, must ask where he came from, why he is here, and where he is going; must say "Does death end all? When we die do we cease to be, and is that probably the end of us forever?" Every man must ask these questions, and must answer them in some way, or have come to the conclusion that they cannot be answered. We do not say that he must think of these questions long enough or steadily enough to come to clear, definite conclusions with respect to them—in fact, comparatively few, it would seem, do—but that in some vague way, at least, he does think of them, and has, therefore, thoughts of real and practical importance, to him, concerning them. In other words, the fact of being involves believing something. The necessity rests on us all of having a belief of some sort. And not only must every man think, but he must think within the limitations of human thought. There is no such thing as absolutely "free thought." Every man is not only obliged to think but to think within certain defined limits. Within these limitations, however, there is room for the most different conclusions. Still, the alternatives are not numerous. We must be theists, or atheists, or agnostics; must either believe in God, or not believe in Him, or come to the conclusion that it is a question that cannot certainly be determined one way or the other, or that the knowledge of Him so transcends the power of human thought that we cannot come to any certain conclusion as to Him, or affirm anything with respect to Him.

One thing, however, is certain, and that is that our belief, whatever it may be, has to do with our conduct, and so with character, and therefore with our destiny. Belief determines actions. If a man believes that the day will be hot or cold he will govern himself accordingly. That which he will plan to do in the one case will not be that which he will plan to do in the other. We know that in all the common affairs of life a man's belief has to do with what he thinks and says and does. It is just as certain also that a man's belief or misbelief or unbelief in God will have to do with that which he thinks and says and does. It is, then, the blindest folly to think that it is of no importance what we believe. Every sane man knows that it is.

We know that in all the ordinary affairs of life our beliefs are not only important but of very great importance. Nor can it be otherwise as to a man's belief, misbelief or unbelief in God.

He has, must have, "a working theory" of life of some sort. If he believes that there is no

God, or that even if there be, he neither has nor can have, any certain convictions as to who He is, or as to His relation to us or our relationship to Him, he will live as if without God in the world.

He may not be a bad man but his will be an earth-bound life. At the best it will be fragmentary, cabined and cramped within the narrow limits of our present brief and uncertain existence. It will not be after the power of an endless life.

It is no less certain that if a man believes, really believes, in a good and loving God who is the Father of us all; in a God who not only knows us but cares for us, can help and does help us; certainly if he believes that God has revealed Himself to us in Jesus Christ His Son our Lord; that "our Saviour Jesus Christ hath brought life and immortality to light through the gospel;" that in Him we have knowledge of privilege, duty and destiny, such belief has, and must have to do with conduct, with character, and so with destiny. There can be no doubt about it. Observation and history—the history of the world for now eighteen hundred years— tell us that it is so. And this the voice of conscience confirms. Whether men acknowledge it or not they live in the light of a certain "looking for of judgment." St. Paul knew that there is that in every man which would witness to the truth of his words when he said, "Every one of us shall give account of himself to God."

II.

ATHEISM AND AGNOSTICISM.

2 TIM. i. 12.

II.

ATHEISM AND AGNOSTICISM.

IT is enough to say of atheism that it is only a theory. In the nature of the case it can never be anything more than that. It is incapable of proof. It is irreconcilable with indisputable facts. It accounts for nothing. It explains nothing. As a working theory it breaks down on the first test and fails on every further trial. It does not lessen, it only increases, the mystery of existence. As long as a theory does that, it never can seriously rival one that vastly lessens the mystery. The presumptions are all against it as long as it sheds no ray of light on the dark problem of life, but only shrouds it in a thicker darkness. In other words, the atheistic theory is unscientific in that it does not reduce the problem of life to its simplest and lowest terms. Nor does agnosticism do so any more successfully. It is, in fact, only a milder-mannered atheism. Atheism is an ugly word. It has an ill name; has long been in bad repute; has long been associated in men's minds with some of the most tragic events in human history. Few men would willingly be known as atheists; none of the better sort. We have, however, in these latter days the same thing under another name. Agnosticism is another, although milder, form of atheism. It admits that the contention of the dogmatic atheist is untenable. But practically it comes to like conclusions and influences character and conduct in identically the same way. It tries to obliterate from the mind any distinction between knowing in part and knowing perfectly. It is true that in a sense, we are all agnostics; that in religion as in everything, the known stretches off into the unknown; that there is that in the Infinite of which we now know little or nothing at all, and doubtless that which we can never know. And yet because we do not know everything, it does not follow that we do not know anything, or that what we do know is not of the utmost importance to us. It might as well be said that because we do not know what electricity is, therefore we know nothing about it, or that what we do know is of no practical value. It is not necessary to say that our present knowledge of God is partial, in a sense imperfect, and that the finite never can adequately know the Infinite. We can never comprehend God, but we can and do apprehend Him as "God the Father Almighty, Maker of heaven and earth." There is a vast difference between apprehension and comprehension.

Every one can apprehend the fact that Mr. Herbert Spencer is the great apostle of agnosticism, and that he is the author of various works "in which are some things hard to be understood." As for example, he tells us that the present universe has been evolved by "a change from an indefinite, incoherent homogeneity to a definite, coherent heterogeneity through continuous differentiations and integrations."

There are, of course, those who understand perfectly well what he means, yet, doubtless, to the many these words of his are utterly unintelligible. But because they do not understand him in this instance, it does not follow that it is always the case. His incomprehensibility does not destroy for them his intelligibility. The agnostic tell us that although there must be a First Cause, which, if we choose, we may call God, yet that He is, and in the nature of the case must be, both unknown and unknowable. If we ask, why? we are told that the finite cannot comprehend the Infinite, and that the knowledge of the Infinite and Unconditioned transcends all human thought. And so the agnostic claims that we neither know, nor can know, anything as to the being or nature of God; that we have no right to assign to Him any attribute or quality whatsoever, good or bad; that the Unknown and Unknowable need not, and, in fact should not concern us one way or the other; that what we do or refrain from doing, may be of importance to us and to other men, but that we have no reason for supposing that it can concern God. We are, in fact, told that we have no right to speak of "the unknown God" as Him or It, or attribute to God either personality or any other quality or characteristic whatsoever.

Agnosticism is therefore destructive not only of religion but of morals as well. If its argument is good for anything, it must be for everything. If it is valid against what the Christian Faith tells us of God, then it must be equally valid against knowledge of every sort; for, turn to what field of knowledge or point of observation we will, it is still the same; the known soon stretches off into the unknown, the illimitable, the transcendent. And yet on this ground to deny the validity and value of our knowledge is to commit intellectual suicide and bring in universal scepticism. No: the Christian has no need to be troubled by the atheistic or agnostic boasting of our time.

The established facts of our modern sciences have in no way weakened the foundations of the Christian Faith. With full knowledge of all that the wise of this world have said, or now say, the Christian of to-day can, with all the confidence that thrilled the soul of the great Apostle of old, say, "I know whom I have believed, and am persuaded that He is able to keep that which I have committed unto Him against that day." No thoughtful, certainly no earnest man, can long bear the burden of either atheism or agnosticism. The atheist looks into the mystery of life and says that it neither has nor can have any solution, and, though the agnostic is not quite so dogmatic still he maintains that even if there is a God He is inscrutable, unknown and unknowable.

And so, on the atheist and on the agnostic alike rests the awful burden of an unintelligible world.

III.

OF BELIEF IN GOD.

Heb. xi. 6.

III.

OF BELIEF IN GOD.

IN instructing her child in the "things which a Christian ought to know and believe to his soul's health" the Church teaches him, first of all to say—"I believe in God, the Father Almighty, Maker of heaven and earth." It is the first article of that Faith which is the universal creed of Christendom. Not only do all Christians believe in God, but, in some sense, it is the belief of well-nigh all human kind. There are indeed atheists, but they are comparatively few, so few as hardly to be taken into the account. Making due allowance for them, it may still be said that, in general, belief in God is the common conviction of men. The first article of the Creed more than any other meets the test of St. Vincent of Lerins—*Quod semper, quod ubique, quod ab omnibus*—for not only is it believed by absolutely all Christians, but by well-nigh all men. It comes to us with all the impressiveness of a universal conviction. And this fact invests the belief with the most profound significance. There may be those to whom this universality of the belief is of no importance, but the man who can jauntily set aside a well-nigh universal conviction of his fellow-

men is not one to waste words with. The only
hope for such a man is that he will some day
come to have a human heart. To every thoughtful man belief in God is one of the most significant characteristics of men; and it is that which
every thoughtful man will at least try to account
for. To Christians it was adequately accounted
for by St. Paul, when, in addressing the heathen
of Lystra, he said of God that "He left not Himself without witness, in that He did good, and
gave us rain from heaven, and fruitful seasons,
filling our hearts with food and gladness;" and
by St. John, when he said of Jesus Christ, our
Lord: "That was the true Light, which lighteth every man that cometh into the world." But
these, and the many like words of Holy Scripture,
weigh with Christians only. To unbelievers it
is useless to quote even such texts as these that
witness to this universal Faith, because for them
the words of Scripture, however reasonable, go
for nothing. I do not therefore, dwell on what
the Bible has to say. It is a significant thing
that the Bible enters into no argument as to the
being of God. It simply declares that He is;
says: "In the beginning God created the heaven
and the earth." But because the Bible does not
argue the question, it does not follow that we
should not. If we think at all we must think of
this greatest of all questions. We encounter
everywhere this conviction of men that God is.
It is a universal Faith. It has no formidable

rival. It has the field; has had it and held it all along. How and why? We must have some rationale of the fact. The presumption is that this belief has obtained because it ought to, because it is far more reasonable than any other; that it is an example of "the survival of the fittest" Faith. Our belief, like our knowledge, is largely a matter of inheritance, but neither the one nor the other would last long on tradition only or chiefly. It is certain that man's belief in God rests on convictions and reasons, reasons which have seemed good and sufficient to the successive generations since the world began; reasons which seem good and sufficient still to a vast, an overwhelming, majority of human kind.

These reasons are convincing and well known: too well known to need rehearsal.

They are chiefly the argument from causation; from the order and from the countless adaptations of the universe, and from the moral nature of man. *Nothing has been evolved that was not involved.* Everywhere in Nature we find law and order, thought and purpose, exhaustless adaptation, and a correlation of things on a scale of limitless extent and transcendent power. But above all man himself is the marvel of the world.

He is conscious of himself and of his free moral agency—that he is not a thing but a person. And from the personality of man we must infer the personality of God. Consciousness cannot be the outcome of unconsciousness.

Nor is it possible that the personality and moral nature of man could have originated in anything less than the personality and moral nature of God. Without God, man and the universe are alike inexplicable, and this has moved the vast majority of men to join in saying—"I believe in God, the Father Almighty, Maker of heaven and earth."

IV.

HOW GOD IS KNOWN.

St. John i. 18.

HOW GOD IS KNOWN.

"NO man hath seen God at any time." On this fact is founded one of the most common cavils of unbelievers of a certain sort. It is said: "Why should you expect me to believe in God? I never saw Him; you never saw Him; no man ever saw Him." An infidel orator has said: "I have lived in the world for fifty years and more, and I never yet saw God; show Him to me and I will believe in Him." A moment's reflection will show the folly of such talk. We believe in many things that no man hath seen or can see. We believe in electricity. We have never seen it. We do not know what it is. But we know how it acts, and so can make it do our bidding. We believe in life, in death, in our mind, our affections, our hopes and fears, our likes and dislikes. These, however, no man hath seen or can see, and yet to deny them would be an indication of insanity or idiocy. Suppose that instead of saying, "No man hath seen God," you say, "No man hath seen me." Both assertions are true. No man hath seen me. The I, the real self, is an unseen and yet real existence. You see a man's face and figure, but never the

man himself, that unseen, spiritual being, who
thinks, loves, hopes, fears, sins, and sorrows.
We talk of seeing each other, and yet we really
never do see each other. It is said: "Did you
see Mr. Blank yesterday?" And you answer
yes or no, as the case may be. But the fact is
you never really saw him, and in this world, at
least, you never will. With profound significance it was said: "Now we see through a glass
darkly; but then face to face; now I know in
part; but then shall I know even as also I am
known." Socrates said: "You can bury me if
you can catch me;" and truly. You cannot
bury me. You may bury my body, but my body
is mine, not me. You say that a man is dead.
But all that you mean by it is that he is no
longer knowable to you through the senses. His
body has fallen out of correspondence with its
environment. It is the body that is dead. You
have no right to say that the man himself is.
Plainly no man hath seen himself or any other
man. But this in no way invalidates the reality
of our knowledge. We know that we exist because we are conscious that we do. We say that
a man is unconscious, that is, that for the time
he does not know that he exists. To be perma-
nently unconscious would simply be annihilation.
Our own existence is not a matter of belief but
of knowledge. We know that we exist because
we are conscious that we do. But we cannot in
that way know that other men exist. How then

do we know it? By inference. We see their face and form; see their acts and hear their words in and through their bodily organs. We are conscious that we act in certain ways, and so we infer that they do also. That is, our knowledge of other men is not direct, immediate knowledge but inferential: and intellectually we know God in the same way: that is, inferentially; by necessary indubitable inference. It is not, indeed, our only way of knowing God, but the rational process of knowing Him. We know Him in manifold ways; by intuition; by a conviction that He is and has to do with us and we with Him; through our needs, our affections, our hopes and fears; through the deep, undying necessities of our soul's life. Above all we know God through Jesus Christ His Son our Lord.

In the incarnation God made Himself accessible to men; looked on them through human eyes; spake to them in a human voice, and through the deep, undying necessities of our soul's life. In the words of a great teacher (Liddon), "Jesus is the Almighty, restraining His illimitable powers; Jesus is the Incomprehensible, voluntarily submitting to bonds; Jesus is Providence, clothed in our own flesh and blood; Jesus is the Infinite Charity, tending us with the kindly looks and tender handling of a human love; Jesus is the Eternal wisdom, speaking out of the depths of infinite thought in a human language. Jesus is God making Himself, if I may dare so to speak, our tangible possession; He is God brought 'very nigh to us, in our mouth and in our heart'; we behold Him, we touch Him, we cling to Him, and lo! we are partakers of the Nature of Deity, through our actual membership in His body, in His flesh, and in His bones; we dwell, if we will, evermore in Him, and He in us."

V.

GOD THE CREATOR.

GEN. i. 1.

V

GOD THE CREATOR.

WE know that we exist. We are conscious of it. We unhesitatingly believe in the existence of other men, and in certain things with respect to them. It is a matter of belief, not of knowledge; but it is none the less a matter of certitude. It is firmly founded on a process of reasoning, of inference. And it is in identically the same way that we come to believe in Almighty God and in certain things with respect to Him. The creed of Christendom teaches us to say: "I believe in God the Father Almighty, Maker of heaven and earth." Christians believe God to be "Our Father," because Jesus Christ our Lord has thus revealed Him to us. But all men—well nigh all men—believe in God as the Maker of heaven and earth, and this universal conviction rests on indubitable inference. We see that all things around us existed first of all ideally. It is impossible to think of a chair apart from a chair-maker. We know that it first existed in the mind of the man who made it. Its outward visible form is the sign of its inward spiritual origin. Before there ever was a chair there was a chair-maker, and but for a chair-maker there never would have been a chair. The chair is proof of a chair-maker. Every made thing witnesses to a maker. Nor does this hold good only as regards man-made things, for matter cannot do anything. It cannot think or act. It is passive, acted upon. We therefore unhesitatingly conclude that the worlds could not have made themselves, and that they are not the result of chance or accident. Thought implies a thinker. They must have had a Maker. It is not a mere supposition. It is a necessary conclusion. Herbert Spencer gives expression to a universal conviction in saying that "The assumption of the existence of a first cause of the universe is a necessity of thought." In other words, the existence of the Creator is not a possibility or probability. It is a "necessity of thought." We are obliged to believe in a first cause. The universe is not a cause. It is caused. Creation is simply a fact, a present on-going process. We lift up our eyes and see it everywhere around us. The worlds were brought to their present condition. They have certainly had a cause, and a cause adequate to their production. They are of countless number. They move in an unerring order. They are held in an Omnipotent Hand. In this the reasoning of St. Paul is as good to-day as when he said of the Creator: "The invisible things of Him from the creation of the world are clearly seen, being understood by the things that are made, even His eternal power and Godhead."

In this, at least, Mr. Spencer, the very Coryphæus of modern agnosticism, agrees with St. Paul in insisting that "The assumption of the existence of a first cause of the universe is a necessity of thought." And, since this first cause—whom Christians call "Our Father in heaven"—is seen to be of almighty power, the universal conviction of men finds expression in that article of the Christian Faith wherein we are taught to say—"I believe in God the Father Almighty, Maker of heaven and earth." Christians believe Him to be our Father because Jesus Christ our Saviour has thus revealed Him to men; but all that we are now insisting on is that all men, whether Christians or not, must believe Him to be the Maker of heaven and earth.

It is hardly necessary to say that our opinion as to the method of creation is another matter altogether. It is not of the Faith; it is not definitely revealed in Holy Scripture, and not so much as mentioned in the Creed. What the Bible does most unmistakably assert is that "God created the heaven and the earth;" and this is all that we are asked to believe herein. A Christian may, if he will, think the world created in six days, or six years, or sixty million years. It matters not. What he is required to believe is that God created the heaven and the earth.

As Baronius saith: "The intention of Scripture is to tell us how to go to heaven; not to show us how the heaven goeth," and, as St. Paul says, it "is profitable for doctrine, for reproof, for correction, for instruction in righteousness." It was never meant to be profitable for instruction in chemistry, astronomy, geology, and the like.

The Christian Faith does not pledge us to any particular theory as to the method or manner of creation, but it does teach us to say—"I believe in God the Father Almighty, Maker of heaven and earth, and of all things visible and invisible."

VI.

AN OBJECTION CONSIDERED.

PSALM xix. 7.

VI.

AN OBJECTION CONSIDERED.

WE are so constituted that we are obliged to believe that every effect has a cause adequate to its production; and since the universe is not a cause but an effect, we are obliged to believe that it had its origin in a cause adequate to its production. Even Herbert Spencer admits that: "The assumption of the existence of a first cause of the universe is a necessity of thought." In so far, he is at one with the Christian theist, since to say that "The assumption of the existence of a first cause of the universe is a necessity of thought," is only another way of saying that the existence of God is a necessity of thought. But we hear it said: "Why are we obliged to come to the conclusion of the Christian Theist or of Mr. Spencer either? Why not suppose the universe the outcome of the blind forces that are in Nature?" Because it is a mere supposition, and an utterly unreasonable one. It does not in any way lessen the mystery of the origin of things. It accounts for nothing. It does not in any way account for "the forces that are in Nature." It ascribes to them power or powers, whereas we know that they are merely manifestations of power. Then, too, it involves the absurdity of supposing that the effect is greater than the supposed cause; that intelligence is the product of non-intelligence; that that has been evolved which is not involved. To say that the universe is the outcome of the forces or laws of Nature is a mere sophism. A "law of Nature" is in no sense a cause of anything. It does nothing, can do nothing. The will of the Almighty Power that orders all things is manifested to us in a certain invariable order, and observing this order we speak of it as a "law of Nature," but we should remember that this is a mere figure of speech. In the same way we speak of the law as doing this and that. But in truth it does nothing, can do nothing. We say that the law of the commonwealth hangs for murder, and sends the thief to prison. But what we really mean is that the people who make the law do this.

The laws of the commonwealth are simply the rules which the people have agreed to carry out. The police, the judge, the jury, act simply as the agents of the sovereign people. The laws are simply a record of certain rules which the people have established for their guidance. And it is to be remembered that these laws do not enforce themselves. In fact they do nothing at all. The people make the laws, and having made them they enforce them. And this is equally true as regards these so-called laws of Nature. They do nothing. A "law of Nature" is simply the orderly manifestation of His righteous rule whose never-failing providence ordereth all things in heaven and earth. No less is freely admitted by Mr. John Fiske, in saying: " To the scientific investigator, as such, the forces of nature are doubtless blind, like the x and y in algebra, but this is only so long as he contents himself with describing their modes of operation. When he undertakes to explain them philosophically he can in nowise dispense with his theistic hypothesis."

It should never be forgotten that "a law of Nature" does nothing and explains nothing. It is only a summary of the facts to be explained, a statement of the way in which things happen. Thus, the law of gravitation is the fact that all material bodies attract one another, with a force varying directly with their mass, and inversely with the square of their distance. But the fact that bodies attract one another in this way, cannot be explained by the law; for the fact is the law, and the law is the fact. To say that the gravitation of matter is accounted for by the law of gravitation is merely to say that matter gravitates because it gravitates. And so of the other laws of Nature ; which taken together, are the expression, in a set of convenient formulæ, of all the facts of our experience. The so-called laws of Nature are merely the facts of Nature summarized. To say, then, that Nature is explained by law, is to say that the facts are explained by themselves, which is an absurdity. The question then remains, Why are the facts what they are?

And there are only two possible answers. They are what they are either as the result of mere chance, or through purpose, the will of God, "Whose never-failing Providence ordereth all things in heaven and earth." That they are the result of chance no sane man can suppose. It is unthinkable. We are therefore shut up to the other alternative, namely, that they are what they are through purpose,—the will of God. The "laws of Nature" are in reality the Divine constitution which God's will has given to things and persons: and of the will of God, however made known to us, we may well say with the Psalmist:

"The law of the Lord is an undefiled law, converting the soul: the testimony of the Lord is sure, and giveth wisdom unto the simple.

"The statutes of the Lord are right, and rejoice the heart: the commandment of the Lord is pure, and giveth light unto the eyes.

"The fear of the Lord is clean, and endureth forever: the judgments of the Lord are true, and righteous altogether.

"More to be desired are they than gold, yea, than much fine gold: sweeter also than honey, and the honeycomb.

"Moreover, by them is thy servant taught: and in keeping of them there is great reward."

VII.

THE WISDOM AND POWER OF GOD.

PSALM cxxxix. 12.

VII.

THE WISDOM AND POWER OF GOD.

ASIDE from anything that revealed religion teaches, there are certain common conclusions which men have arrived at with respect to God; and this belief—like belief in our fellowmen—is founded on inference. It is a result of reasoning from the known to the unknown; from the seen and temporal to the unseen and eternal. We know that we are here; that the world is here; that the universe stretches everywhere around us; that we and this whole seen universe belong to the realm of created things, and had a Creator. As Mr. Herbert Spencer admits: "The assumption of the existence of a first cause of the universe is a necessity of thought;" and as Mill confesses, "The argument for a first cause admits of being and is presented as a conclusion from the whole of human experience."

This first cause we call God. We believe that "It is He that hath made us, and not we ourselves." We believe Him to be the "Maker of all things visible and invisible." Now from His works what can we infer with respect to Him? When a man shows us the works that his hands have made we infer certain things as to the man himself. If his works exhibit thought, wisdom, foresight, we unhesitatingly conclude that these qualities characterize the man himself. In identically the same way we draw certain inferences with respect to God. We see everywhere throughout the universe manifestations of a practically almighty power. On this we found our belief in the omnipotence of God. Further, we see everywhere around us manifestations of the most surpassing knowledge, thought, wisdom, foresight, the most wonderful adaptation of means to the accomplishment of desired ends. We observe everywhere how things quite separate and distinct in themselves are correlated the one to the other for the production of certain results which would otherwise have been impossible. Thus, we find men endowed with organs of speech and hearing, an elaborate and wonderfully adapted mechanism most admirably suited to answer a specific purpose. But neither the organs of speech nor of hearing would be of the least possible avail but for the air we breathe, which acts as a conductor of sound, thus making speech and hearing possible. Here we have three entirely distinct things, each serving a certain necessary purpose, and each absolutely necessary to a certain result. And such adjustments, adaptations, and correlations exist everywhere throughout the universe in inconceivable number and to an inconceivable extent.

No man can reasonably believe them to be the

result of chance. No man can reasonably believe them to be the outcome of blind, unintelli-
gent forces. In fact, so far as we know, no such
forces exist. It is quite unreasonable to think
that there are any such forces.

No, these marvelous adaptations and correlations are manifestations of the Infinite thought,
wisdom, foresight, and power. And as all these
are seen on so vast a scale throughout the universe, and may reasonably be thought to exist
on a still vaster scale beyond our powers of observation and knowledge, they are manifestations
not only of the infinite power but of the infinite
knowledge and wisdom of God. Furthermore,
we know that these are attributes of personality.
They do not inhere in inanimate things. Thought
implies a thinker, and a thinker is a person. And,
since we see the manifestations of thought everywhere throughout the universe, we are inferentially led to believe not only in the infinite
power and wisdom of God but in His personality
as well.

He is the living God with whom we have to
do now and here and forever: "in whom we
live and move and have our being." That we
may learn a lesson as to His Divine presence,
personality and power well may we Christians
of these latter days listen to the lesson of that
Psalmist of old time who said:

"O Lord, Thou hast searched me out, and
know me: Thou knowest my down-sitting, and

mine up-rising; Thou understandest my thoughts long before.

"Thou art about my path, and about my bed: and spiest out all my ways.

"For lo, there is not a word in my tongue: but Thou, O Lord, knowest it altogether.

"Thou hast fashioned me behind and before: and laid Thine hand upon me.

"Such knowledge is too wonderful and excellent for me: I cannot attain unto it.

"Whither shall I go then from Thy Spirit: or whither shall I go then from Thy presence?

"If I climb up into heaven, Thou art there: if I go down to hell, Thou art there also.

"If I take the wings of the morning: and remain in the uttermost parts of the sea;

"Even there also shall Thy hand lead me: and Thy right hand shall hold me.

"If I say, Peradventure the darkness shall cover me: then shall my night be turned to day.

"Yea, the darkness is no darkness with Thee, but the night is as clear as the day: the darkness and light to Thee are both alike.

"For my reins are Thine: Thou hast covered me in my mother's womb.

"I will give thanks unto Thee, for I am fearfully and wonderfully made: marvelous are Thy works, and that my soul knoweth right well."

VIII.

IS GOD GOOD?

1 JOHN, iv. 16.

VIII.

IS GOD GOOD?

FEW, if any, will deny the assertion of Herbert Spencer that "The assumption of the existence of a first cause of the universe is a necessity of thought," or disagree with Mill in saying that "The argument for a first cause admits of being and is presented as a conclusion from the whole of human experience." This first cause men call God. His marvelous knowledge, wisdom, foresight, and power are seen in His works. These attributes are witnessed to on so vast a scale that we are justified in regarding them as infinite. That belief in such a being is matter of great importance no thoughtful man will deny. That we always have to do with Him; are always in the presence of His infinite knowledge and almighty power; that "in Him we live and move and have our being," is certainly a matter to be very seriously considered; hence the vast importance of faith in the nature, the character, of God; of asking, "How will He exercise His almighty power?" Will it be for our good? Does He really care anything for us? Is He mindful of us? Are we safe in His hands? What assurance have we that we are? Belief in

His omnipotence is, of itself, not very satisfying. It might lead us to fear God. It never would move us to love Him. The heathen of old felt this keenly. It caused them to propitiate Him when they thought He was angry with them; to try to purchase His favor with costly gifts, and even with human sacrifices, but they never thought of loving God. And if He is the pitiless Doom of Mohammedanism, or even as some Christian theologians have represented Him to be—if as the Confession of Faith of the Westminster Assembly asserts, He cares only for a favored few, and "The rest of mankind God was pleased, according to the unsearchable counsel of His own will, whereby He extendeth or withholdeth mercy as He pleaseth, for the glory of His sovereign power over His creatures, to pass by, and to ordain them to dishonor and wrath for their sin, to the praise of His glorious justice"—we would have good cause to fear Him. In such case, however, it would not seem possible to love Him, or indeed for a just or a merciful man to help feeling toward Him the very opposite of love.

No, it is not enough to believe in the omniscience and the omnipotence of God. If we are to love Him we must have some further faith in Him. We must believe Him to be lovable; must believe in His goodness. Is God good? It is not a presumptuous or irreverent inquiry. It is a very necessary one. It is not only right but our duty to make it; for it would be a wrong thing to love God if He is not lovable. Is He lovable? The question should be asked not only in the interest of true religion but of morals as well. Is it capable of an altogether satisfactory answer? It would not seem so if our belief must rest simply on what we see in the world around us, and are obliged to infer from what we see only. We see a great deal that would lead us to infer that God is good; that He is mindful of us and would fain promote our well-being and happiness. We find ourselves in a beautiful world, marvelously provided not only with all things necessary to our existence, but with a vast number of things evidently meant to minister to our satisfaction, comfort, and pleasure.

This, however, is not all that we find, by any means. We find pestilence, famine, hideous diseases, countless forms of rapine and of suffering, and seemingly a great deal of unnecessary misery. In every drop of water we see the pursuer and the pursued, the destroyer and the destroyed. Nature makes the maw of the shark and the blade of the sword-fish, and seems to care no more for the lamb than for the lion. It arms man and beast for rapine and plunder. The lair of the lion is strewn with the bones of its victims, the eagle's beak is red with blood, and its talons clotted with the feathers of the dove. If we look to nature only for an an-

swer to our inquiry, we will not find one that
can satisfy us. It does not tell us whether the
power behind nature is tender, pitiful, kind and
just. It is no wonder that those who refuse to
believe that God has made any other revelation
than that which nature tells of, are led to doubt
either the infinite love or the infinite power of
God.

From his standpoint it seemed an inevitable
conclusion to Mill. He says: "These then are
the net results of natural theology on the question of the Divine attributes: a being of great
but limited power, how or by what limited we
cannot even conjecture; of great and perhaps
unlimited intelligence, but perhaps also more
limited than His power; who desires and pays
some regard to the happiness of His creatures,
but who seems to have other motives of action
which He cares more for, and who can hardly be
supposed to have created the universe for that
purpose alone. Such is the Deity whom natural
religion points to; and any idea of God more
captivating than this comes from human wishes,
or from the teaching of either real or imaginary
revelation." The most that he can say is that
"There is a preponderance of evidence that the
Creator desired the pleasure of His creatures,"
and again, that "There is much appearance that
pleasure is agreeable to the Creator, while there
is very little if any appearance that pain is so,
and there is a certain amount of justification for

inferring, on the ground of natural theology alone, that benevolence is one of the attributes of the Creator." (Theism, p. 195.) This was the deliberate conclusion of a cold, cautious, but candid thinker, whose early training had prejudiced him not only against religion in general, but against Christianity in particular. This, however, is to be said for him: He had identified Christianity with the Calvinistic theology, and rejecting the one rejected the other also. Not seeing in Jesus Christ the manifestation of God, coming to his conclusions only from what he saw in the world around him, he could not believe in the infinite power and in the infinite goodness of God. Nor is it plain how any one can, unless he believes in Jesus Christ as the manifestation of God to man. When once we believe in Him, and that He was what He affirmed Himself to be, and what the Church Catholic has always confessed concerning Him, then, and then only, can we believe in the infinite goodness of God, and that there was nothing, consistent with the infinite perfection of His nature, that He would not do and endure and suffer " for us men and for our salvation."

IX.

REVELATION IN GENERAL.

Acts x. 34, 35.

REVELATION IN GENERAL.

THE argument from Natural Theology is not to be despised; neither should it be taken for more than it is worth. It does something for us, yes, a good deal. It witnesses to the existence, the wisdom, the might, the majesty of God; tells us that the Creator is a being of seemingly infinite intelligence and power, that He cares for us, for our well-being and happiness. It fails, however, fully to assure us of the infinite goodness, the infinite loveliness of God. After stating "the net results of Natural Theology on the question of the Divine attributes," Mill says "Any idea of God more captivating than this comes from human wishes, or from the teaching of either real or imaginary revelation." We neither deny his conclusion nor question his statement.

Christians, however, are not confined to his disheartening "net results." They believe not only in the infinite power, but in the infinite goodness of God, because they believe in Jesus Christ as "God manifest in the flesh." In this faith they believe that "God is love," that there was nothing that He would not do, nothing that

63

He would not endure or suffer "for us men and for our salvation." This involves revelation. Revelation is a fact, not a theory. Men have ingeniously argued the probability of a revelation; that it is that which we would expect in view of the character of God and the condition of man. There is great force in what they have urged. We would certainly infer that if we needed help, a friend would help us if he could. Should a man refuse to help us when he could we would certainly infer that he is not friendly to us. It is a reasonable inference. No man would fail to make it. Nor is it any the less reasonable as applied to our relationship to God. We certainly need more light shed upon our darkness than Natural Theology bestows. Our need herein is so urgent that we must infer that if God is good He would help us if He could. Had He failed to do so we would have been obliged to infer, with Mill, either that He is of "great but limited power," or that "He seems to have other motives of action which He cares more for" than He does for our welfare. But we need not bring forward arguments to show the probability of a revelation, because we have it. We do not argue as to the probability of sunshine when we walk in it, and experience the comfort of its genial light and warmth. And so we need not talk of the probability of a revelation of and from God. We have it. We are here; the world is here; the universe stretches every-

where around us. We are creatures. "It is He
that made us, and not we ourselves." The world
is the work of a Creator. Man witnesses to his
Maker. We are surrounded everywhere with
His works. They are in themselves a revelation. They testify of Him; tell us much concerning Him. Kant spoke for us all in telling
of the prophetic significance of the starry heavens and of the moral law. And these have ever
been elements of the revelation vouchsafed to all
men. Nor have they failed in some wise to
profit by it. The fact is there has always been
a world-wide faith. It has involved belief in a
supreme power or powers; a recognition of human dependence; a belief in the personality of
God; belief that He could help; that He has
helped, and will help. And so men have, everywhere, raised praying hands toward heaven.
More than this, Christians have faith to believe
that Christ is the Light that lighteth all men;
that in every time and place men have had some
measure of light, and that Christ was that light;
that He has, in all times and among all peoples,
as they were able to bear it, been the Divine
Teacher of seer, saint, and sinner.

Even the American savage has a belief, and as
far as it goes, a true faith. He believes in God
as the Great Spirit. He kneels beneath the pines
and prays; and who can doubt but that God is
as ready to hear and to help the poor savage as
He is to hear and help us who rejoice in a fuller

faith. Who can doubt but that the very darkness, the need, the poverty, of the poor savage, constitute an additional claim upon the loving pity of Him who is the God and Father of us all, or that a prayer-hearing, prayer-answering Lord does not send the poor Indian away blessed and comforted, even as He does us.

Not only does the American Indian believe with us in God as the Great Spirit, but with us also that He hears, helps, rewards, and punishes. And more, he believes with us in a future life and that it is one of reward and of penalty. His creed is not expressed in the terms of the Christian Faith, but in much it agreeth thereto. We say we believe in the life everlasting. He says he believes in a happy hunting-ground beyond the grave, and so, in his simplicity, buries beside his dead the pipes, the bow, and the arrows that were dear to him here, with a vague hope that somehow they are prophetic of good awaiting him there. That is, **the poor savage has a faith, a very real faith, and in** its way, a true faith. It is in substance one with the universal faith of men in God, in Divine help, and in rewards and in penalties here and hereafter. The heathen Indian expresses his faith in one way, the stern old Roman and the cultivated Greek expressed theirs in another, but in substance it was the same belief, and in no small degree not dissimilar to the Christian Faith. Well, therefore, did John Milton say: " The true Christian doctrine is the Divine revelation disclosed in various ages by Christ (though He was not known under that name in the beginning) for the promotion of the glory of God and the salvation of men." No less significantly has John Henry Newman said : "Revelation, properly speaking, is a universal, not a local gift, and the distinction between the Israelites formerly and Christians now, and that of the Heathen, is not that we can, and they cannot, attain to future blessedness, but that the Church of God ever has had, and the rest of mankind never had, authoritative documents of truth and appointed channels of communication with God. The Word and sacraments are characteristics of the elect people of God, but all men have had more or less the guidance of tradition, in addition to those internal notions of right and wrong which the Holy Spirit has put into the hearts of all men."

An inspired Apostle says that "When the Gentiles, which have not the law, do by nature the things contained in the law, these, having not the law, are a law unto themselves : which show the work of the law written in their hearts, their conscience also bearing witness, and their thoughts the meanwhile accusing or else excusing one another : " and, on a notable occasion, still another said : "Of a truth I perceive that God is no respecter of persons : but in every nation he that feareth Him, and worketh righteousness, is accepted with Him."

X.

REVELATION IN PARTICULAR.

DEUT. vi. 4.

X.

REVELATION IN PARTICULAR.

WE claim that revelation is a fact, not a theory; that all things witness to their Maker; that head and heart alike demand a faith, and that certain common convictions have, in fact, constituted a universal faith; that however differently expressed, mixed with error, or debased with superstition, these beliefs never wholly lost their hold on men, or failed to exercise a salutary influence. But the more discerning never thought the consentient opinion or faith wholly satisfactory. It had no adequate foundation. It was not only conjectural, but inadequate in itself and in its power to influence and mould conduct. Something more was very much needed—something more was given. Not only did God in some sense reveal Himself to all men, but so especially to a man and a people. "To Abraham and to his seed were the promises made." To the Father of the Faithful was given a clearer light, a better faith, a holier hope; and this, that "when the fulness of the time was come" it might be Israel's contribution toward the dawn of a new and better day. The revela-

71

tion to the Chosen People was a special revelation of the living God to living men, in its varying stages adapted to the condition and the needs of those to whom it was made. It was educational, gradual, progressive, and necessarily an accommodation to the capacity, the sinfulness, the ignorance, the moral and intellectual state of the successive generations to whom it was given. It involved explicit teaching as to God and His will and desire, necessary discipline, needful correction, and a holy hope, an ever-increasing expectation of far greater blessing yet in store for the people of God. All along, but with ever-increasing particularity, it was associated with the advent of a Person, the Messiah, the Anointed. This from the first was the great hope of Israel. The promise to Moses was: "I will raise up a prophet from among their brethren, like unto thee, and will put My words in his mouth; and he shall speak unto them all that I shall command him; and it shall come to pass that whosoever will not hearken unto My words which He shall speak in My name, I will require it of him."

The mission of Israel was too plain to be misunderstood. Other peoples had their part to fulfil, a part plainly seen by us who have inherited the blessings which they were a means of inaugurating. As clearly as the old Greeks and Romans had their special work to do for the world, so especially had the Chosen People. It

was to bear witness to the one Lord God Almighty; the unity, the spirituality, the morality
of God; His holiness, His goodness, His love.
And this Israel did, however imperfectly; taught
men to believe in a one supreme, living God,
whose never-failing Providence ordereth all
things in heaven and earth; in a one sovereign
Ruler and infallible Judge, who loves good and
hates evil, who rewards the righteous and punishes the guilty. Nor was this all. It was the
part of Israel to nourish and proclaim a better
knowledge and fuller revelation of God. And
this all along was associated with a Person, a
promised Messiah, "the seed of the woman;"
"the seed of Abraham in whom all nations
should be blessed;" "the prophet like unto
Moses, whom the Lord would raise up;" "the
King whom the Lord would set upon His holy
hill;" "the priest after the order of Melchise-
dek;" "the Anointed One;" "the desire of all
nations," who would be "a light to lighten the
Gentiles" as well as "the glory of His people
Israel."

This was their mission, their great contribution
to humankind. And amidst all their sins and
failures, their narrowness, their blindness, their
fanaticism, the Chosen People never lost sight of
their great hope and expectation, and so never
altogether came short of their great mission.
The burden of the Prophets was: "The Lord
whom ye seek shall suddenly come to His temple,

even the Messenger of the Covenant whom ye delight in, but who may abide the day of His coming and who shall stand when He appeareth?"

XI.

THE RECORD OF IT.

ROMANS xiv. 4.

THE RECORD OF IT.

THE record of the revelation, the special revelation made to the Chosen People of old,
is found in the Old Testament. Herein chiefly
consists its inestimable value. It is of course
valuable in many ways. It is a great storehouse
of Oriental antiquities. It is of great value as
history, the record of the rise and progress of a
people, the story of the making of a nation. It
is rich in ethical instruction, in law and literature, in poetry and in politics, but all this is sec-
ondary and incidental. Speaking of these Old
Testament writings an inspired apostle said:
"Whatsoever things were written aforetime were
written for our learning, that we, through patience and comfort of the Scriptures might have
hope," and again tells of them as "profitable for
doctrine, for reproof, for correction, for instruction in righteousness;" not that these Scriptures
are not profitable in many ways, but that herein
lies their greatest value. The Saviour said:
"Search the Scriptures: they are they which
testify of Me." In this consists their inestimable
value. Their great purpose is to testify of Christ.

In remembering this we are saved from endless perplexities.

It is certainly a great mistake for a man to suppose that Christianity is anchored fast to the whole body of Judaism. It is a great mistake to suppose that a Christian is pledged to the acceptance or defence of Judaic opinions, methods, or morals. It is a mistake to lose sight of the fact that revelation has been educational, gradual, progressive, and necessarily suited to the intellectual and moral condition of the successive generations to whom it has been given. The late Frederic Myer, of Keswick, has well described this characteristic of the Old Testament Scriptures. He says: "Not only is there progression in the revelation of the Bible, but also accommodation. By accommodation is meant not merely the use of sensible images and purely human expressions in the conveyance of spiritual ideas, or of types and symbols, and parables and allegories, in the explanation of invisible realities; but more than this; namely, the temporary permission and sanction of existing modes of thought and feeling with regard to religious truth and duty, which were not merely inadequate, but partially untrue, and which it was intended subsequently to supersede by fuller revelations. The earlier anthropomorphic representations of Deity are of this kind; and, indeed, throughout the whole law of Moses, God is spoken of in terms which require a translation into other language with

which the later revelations have furnished us before we can heartily accept them as divine. It
is only, indeed, on this principle of accommodation that we can learn willingly to associate some
portion of the Hebrew Scriptures with the revelation of the Gospel of Christ.

"And when we turn from the region of truth
to that of morality, we find this assumption still
more necessary. We find the polygamy of the
patriarchs, and of David and of Solomon, and the
warrior spirit of the judges, and many acts of
treachery and of cruelty, from Jael to Jehu, sanctioned rather than rebuked by prophetic commu-
nications. . . . So long as the principle of
progression and accommodation in God's revelations is not recognized but rejected, there will
always seem to some a certain measure of rea-
sonableness and healthy moral instinct in the dis-
taste which is felt toward much of the spirit of
Hebrew Scriptures. In such case no explana-
tions or expositions will fail to remove the first
impressions conveyed by the fact of the slaughter
of the Canaanites being said to be in its details
the command of the Most High; or will enable
us to reconcile with the later revelations of Deity
the other suggestions and approvals which we
find ascribed to God in the histories of several of
the judges; or the commands which were given,
and the spirit which was exhibited, by several of
the most conspicuous of the prophets. The exe-
crations of several of the Psalms ever have ap-

peared, and ever will appear, incongruous with
that peculiar spirit of which the Christian is to
be, while many of the habits and practices and
views of the most approved of old time will ob-
viously not bear to be transferred to our conception of any New Testament saint. So long as
we are not permitted to believe that God gave
precepts of duty and revelations of truth to His
people of old only as they could bear them, and
tolerated the coexistence and commingling of
much darkness of the natural man with the special illuminations of His spirit, so long we cannot
but contrast, and contrasting pronounce in many
parts as contradictory, the spirit of the kingdom
which was of this world, and the spirit of that
kingdom which was not of this world; the spirit
of a Joshua, a Samson, or an Elisha, with the
spirit of a Peter, a John, or a Paul."

There are many questions that may be raised
as to these Old Testament Scriptures, but it has
seemed enough, here, only to tell of their one
great purpose, and warn men against burdening
Christianity with endless questions which really
have no necessary relation to Christian believing
and living. The inestimable value of these Old
Testament Scriptures in no way depends on their
supposed errancy or inerrancy in matters not
vital to their one great purpose.

They were given " for doctrine, for reproof, for
correction, for instruction in righteousness : "
and, as the apostle says in another place : " What-

soever things were written aforetime were written for our learning, that we through patience
and comfort of the Scriptures might have
hope."

XII.

JUDAISM IMPERFECT AND TEMPORARY.

GAL. iii. 24.

XII.

REVELATION being a revelation of the living God to living men, it has necessarily been adapted and accommodated to the capacity and condition of those to whom it was made. It has been educational, and therefore gradual and progressive. It would be easy to show this from the Scripture record, but it would take more time and space than the summary plan of these brief papers will allow. Nor can it be very necessary, for the progressive development of doctrine, both in the Old Testament and in the New, can be easily noted and traced by any thoughtful reader of the Scriptures. It is no less evident that from the time of its inauguration Judaism was marked as a temporary system. It was not Catholic, but local and national. It was never meant to be otherwise. It could not be anything else. It was rooted to the soil of a particular country—a narrow, isolated land. The prescribed sacrifices were to be offered at a particular place, in the place which Jehovah should choose "to put His name there." The pilgrimages enjoined on every adult Israelite, three times in the year, were to be at the national altar of his race, and nowhere

else. The appointed times for the observance of
the three great festivals had reference to the
climatic conditions of Judea. They never could
have been made the festivals of a universal religion. The temporary nature of Judaism was
not only implied, but plainly asserted, in the
Hebrew Scriptures. The Zion to which all nations should flow was to be spiritual, not local.
Everything in Judaism was cramped and limited,
and by its very narrowness showed that it was
only for a time. As Barrow has well said:
"God did not by it speak His mind to all, and
so did He not in it speak out all His mind."
"Duties were enjoined that could only be dis-
charged by the Jews; promises were made that
were bounded by the limits of an earthly Canaan;
they were dealt with as children, and led on to
the hope of a present reward, while rebellion was
threatened with a withdrawal of the promised
blessing. But nothing was openly revealed with
respect to a future state of rewards and punish-
ments, and that very defect showed that some
better covenant yet lay hid in the womb of time.
The religion of Judaism was a mere system of
fleshly justification, consisting wholly in matters
of external observance, in washings and purify-
ings, in a costly ritual, and burdensome observ-
ances of times and places; their Passover was a
thanksgiving feast in which the world at large
could never be called to share. The Levitical
tithe to be offered at the national sanctuary

could never be a matter of ecumenic observance. The whole code had a private character, and could no more apply universally than any municipal law could be made a matter of imperial or international obligation. In its ordinances moral duties were sparingly enforced; the devotion of the heart barely indicated; the building up of the inner man as a temple of God mostly ignored; while such things as even heathenism knew to be non-natural to man, polygamy, divorce for any trifling cause, a morose spirit of retaliation and of bloodthirsty revenge, were connived at for the hardness of the Jewish heart, if not sanctioned by positive enactment."— (From the article on Judaism in "Blunt's Dictionary of Doctrinal and Historical Theology.") The revelation made of old time, was good for those to whom it was given; suited to their capacity and to the hardness of men's hearts in that land in those days. But all along there were unmistakable intimations that Judaism was a temporary system, designed to prepare the way for something far better, and suited to the needs of all humankind. "It shall come to pass afterward, that I will pour out My Spirit upon all flesh; and your sons and your daughters shall prophesy, your old men shall dream dreams, your young men shall see visions: and also upon the servants and upon the handmaids in those days will I pour out My Spirit;" and, "Behold, I will send My Messenger, and He shall prepare the way before Me: and the Lord, whom ye seek, shall suddenly come to His temple, even the Messenger of the Covenant, whom ye delight in: behold, He shall come, saith the Lord of Hosts. But who may abide the day of His coming, and who shall stand when He appeareth?"

It is a great mistake to lose sight of the real relation of Judaism to Christianity, or think it necessary for Christians to defend characteristics of a dispensation which was not only not Christian, but in many particulars expressly condemned by Jesus Christ, and clearly cannot be defended on either Christian teaching, or an enlightened modern morality.

Therefore, we here emphasize the fact that Judaism was an imperfect and temporary system; that it most unmistakably bore this stamp from its very inauguration; that in the nature of the case it was largely an adaptation and accommodation to the crude thoughts of a rude age, and to the hard hearts of a stubborn generation. Nor could it have been otherwise, for neither a person nor a people can know more of God than their intellectual and moral condition permits them to know. Judaism had indeed a mission, a great mission. It served its purpose. It was a great bulwark against idolatry. It witnessed to the unity, the spirituality, the holiness of God, and taught men to look forward to a far better and greater day in the coming of that Prophet " of whom Moses in the Law and the Prophets did write." It was well said by Disraeli that "Christianity is the developed religion of the old Israelites. Judaism is that religion suddenly arrested in its growth and petrified."

St. Paul said: "The law was our schoolmaster to bring us unto Christ." And evidently by "the law" he did not mean simply the ten commandments, or the whole body of the Mosaic law, but Judaism as a whole. Of the law taken in this broad and comprehensive sense he asserts that it was a schoolmaster to bring Israel to the Christ, the Lord and Saviour of the world.

XIII.

THE PROMISED MESSIAH.

St. John v. 39.

XIII.

THE PROMISED MESSIAH.

AS Judaism from its inauguration bore the stamp of its imperfect character and temporary purpose, so from the first it led its children to connect "the good things to come," which it shadowed forth, with the advent of the promised Messiah, "the Prophet like unto Moses whom the Lord would raise up." It may be granted that particular texts have been regarded as Messianic on insufficient reason, but it is absolutely certain that the conception of a coming King and Kingdom of God underlies the whole body of prophetic utterances found in the Old Testament Scriptures. From the first there was the general promise of the final triumph over evil; that the seed of the woman would bruise the serpent's heel. Then there was the promise that in the seed of Abraham should "all the nations of the earth be blessed." Then the promise was confined to a single tribe, and to a single family of it. Finally, the time and the very birthplace of the coming Messiah were unmistakably indicated. In many of these prophecies the Messiah was represented in a twofold and seemingly contradictory aspect: at one time as a universal King and Conqueror, whose dominion should cover the earth and endure throughout all ages; and again, as "despised and rejected of men, a man of sorrows and acquainted with grief." The nature of His work, the main characteristics of His life, the very manner of His death and burial, even particular incidents, such as giving Him vinegar to drink, the parting of His raiment, and casting lots for His vesture, had been told in the prophetic utterances. Their evidential value has been well summed up in these words: "The Scriptures of the Old Testament consist of a very varied literature—legal, historical, poetical, prophetic, hortatory, and didactic, the composition of which extended over a period of more than a thousand years; and the books of which it is composed are the works of at least forty different authors; yet, notwithstanding this variety of authorship and dates, the conception of a kingdom of God to be manifested in the future, and of its Messianic King, pervades the whole of them, accompanied with a delineation both of the one and the other, with a distinctness which gradually increases as we descend the stream of time. With respect to these Scriptures, it is a point worthy of careful observation that this Messianic conception existed in the minds of the writers of those books, in the closest union with a profound aspiration for its realization, and a firm belief, notwithstanding every disappointment of their immediate hope,

that it would ultimately be so. A conception of
this kind, and a firm belief in its ultimate realization, are to be found in no other equally varied
literature, extending over an equal interval of
time, and composed by an equal variety of authors. Further: All these prophetical writings
are admitted, even by the most skeptical writers,
to have been composed, with the exception of
the Book of Daniel and a few of the Psalms, not
later than 400 B. C. Briefly stated, the evidential value of these prophetical elements consists
in the fact that they received their realization in
One who was not born until four hundred years
after the last of the prophetic books of the Old
Testament was composed; and that the earnest
aspirations of all the great men who flourished
during these long centuries receive their realization in Him and in Him alone."

He Himself over and over again laid claim to
this witness of the Scriptures concerning Himself; said to those that withstood Him, "Search
the Scriptures; for in them ye think ye have
eternal life: and they are they which testify of
Me:" and to the two that He walked with on
the way to Emmaus, said: "O foolish men,
and slow of heart to believe all that the prophets
have spoken! Ought not Christ to have suffered
these things, and to enter into His glory? And
beginning at Moses, and all the prophets, He
expounded unto them in all the Scriptures the
things concerning Himself." Yes: "God, who

at sundry times and in divers manners spake in times past unto the fathers by the prophets, hath in these last days spoken unto us by His Son, whom He hath appointed heir of all things, by whom also He made the worlds; who being the brightness of His glory, and the express image of His person, and upholding all things by the word of His power, when He had by Himself purged our sins, sat down on the right hand of the Majesty on high; being made so much better than the angels, as He hath by inheritance obtained a more excellent name than they. For unto which of the angels said He at any time, Thou art My Son, this day have I begotten thee? And again, I will be to him a Father, and he shall be to Me a Son? And again, when He bringeth in the first-begotten into the world, He saith, And let all the angels of God worship him."

"God hath spoken unto us by His Son." May we hear, heed, and follow Him. He said: "My sheep hear My voice, and I know them and they follow Me: and I give unto them eternal life; and they shall never perish, neither shall any man pluck them out of My hand."

XIV.

JESUS THE CHRIST.

ST. JOHN xi. 27.

XIV.

JESUS THE CHRIST.

THE best-known name in all the world is that
of Jesus Christ. It would have been better, perhaps, had men learned to speak of Him
as Jesus, the Christ, since the words Jesus Christ
stand more for a name than for a name and an
office; whereas, to speak of Him as Jesus, the
Christ, would not only indicate His name but
witness to His office as the Anointed, the Consecrated One, the One appointed to a unique work,
set apart to an unspeakably important service of
God and man.

To the Jew of old, and even to the pagan,
there could have been no doubt as to the meaning of the word Christ, the Christos, the
Anointed, one representing to him some person
who had been publicly set apart to some great
office among men.

Anointing was the act by which, especially
among the Jews, a man was set apart to some
Divinely appointed office among the people; the
prophet who was to speak from God, the priest
who was to minister to the people in holy things
for God, the king who was to rule in God's glory
over God's own people, were solemnly set apart

99

by anointing to their office. What they would have called anointing we now call consecration, the publicly and Divinely ordered sanctioning and setting apart of a man for an office in which he is to minister unto men and for God. This is anointing, and more than this, it implies that with the appointment and consecration came a power and grace to fit a man for the office he received. Oil, which was in those days, and in that part of the world, a symbol of life and vigor, and communicated strength and health when it was poured on the head of him who was set apart for a public office, implied not merely, "You are thus set apart, but in doing the high office you shall have a special grace and power, an unction from the Holy One, to enable you to do it," and so oil was poured on the head of the anointed one, and ran down his beard, even to the fringes of his garment, signifying life, a consecrated and devoted life. When our Lord, then, is called the Anointed One, the Christ, it means that He is the One of all humanity who is Divinely consecrated and set apart to noble office and high service, and whose whole life and being is filled with the Divine light necessary for doing the work of that office—the anointed, consecrated One in whom all consecration and Divine unction centres for the performance of all offices. And every one of these offices was in the service of mankind. The prophetic office was His, and He claims it as His own when He says, "The

Spirit of the Lord is upon Me for He hath
anointed Me to preach the gospel to the poor."
The prophet's office was an office to serve mankind as their teacher, their guide, and their coun-
sellor. The priestly office was His that He
might offer Himself as a Lamb without spot or
blemish to God, and having entered by a new
and living way with His own blood, should live
for intercession and sacrifice, coming forth with
blessing for God's people. God made Him King
over them, and gave Him heaven for an inheritance that He might rule in righteousness and
peace. Prophet, Priest, and King—in each one
of these was He the servant of mankind, as He
said—" the Son of man came not to be ministered
unto, but to minister, and to give His life a ransom
for many." This is the idea of the Anointed
One, the Christ of God.

And that Jesus regarded Himself as such needs
no proof. It is the key to all that He said and
did. As in the synagogue at Nazareth He read
the magnificent Messianic prophecy of Elias, He
said: "This day is the Scripture fulfilled in your
ears;" that is, He unhesitatingly asserted His
Messiahship, His right to speak "as one having
authority;" to declare the things needful for
men to know, and necessary for men to be and
to do. In short, He asserted and exercised His
right to speak for God and man; to reveal to
men their relation to God and to each other; to
tell them of their origin, their duty, their destiny.

As the Christ, He regarded Himself not only as
the Prophet but as the Priest and King of men.
As Priest, He said that He " came not to be ministered unto but to minister and to give His life
a ransom for many;" that "as Moses lifted up
the serpent in the wilderness even so must the
Son of Man be lifted up, that whosoever believeth in Him should not perish but have eternal
life."   As King, He hesitated not to exercise all
kingly authority and functions; not indeed, as
King of a poor, perishable kingdom, but of an
imperishable, spiritual, and eternal.   In fact, His
Kingly power covers not only this life and world,
but all worlds, and every created intelligence.
He said, "All power is given unto Me in heaven
and in earth."   As King of kings and Lord of
lords He made the most exclusive claims, the
most peremptory demands, and exercised the
most supreme prerogatives.   He allowed no
other claim to rival His; said, " He that loveth
father or mother more than Me, is not worthy
of Me; and he that loveth son or daughter
more than Me is not worthy of Me;" and "I
am the resurrection, and the life; he that
believeth in Me, though he were dead yet shall
he live; and whosoever liveth and believeth in
Me shall never die."   In other words, He is the
Christ here and everywhere and forever: "Jesus,
the Christ, the same yesterday, to-day, and forever."

XV.

THE FULFILLER OF THE LAW AND THE PROPHETS.

St. Matt. v. 17.

XV.

THE FULFILLER OF THE LAW AND THE PROPHETS.

WE find in the gospels ample evidence that to those who first heard it the teaching of Jesus Christ seemed new and strange, not to say startling. "The people were astonished at His doctrine; for He taught as one having authority and not as the scribes." The scribes and Pharisees regarded His teaching as not only new and strange but as pernicious, revolutionary, subversive of the Law and the Prophets, and of everything that was dearest—to them. Knowing their thoughts Jesus said: "Think not that I am come to destroy the Law, or the Prophets: I am not come to destroy, but to fulfil." Naturally, those suspicious and narrow hierarchs did not believe Him: nor did even those that loved Him know what He meant. "These things understood not the disciples at the first." It was only "when Jesus was glorified" that they perceived that He had indeed fulfilled the Law and the Prophets. How did He do it? He fulfilled the Law not only by conforming to the spirit as well as the letter of its requirements, but by living a life of absolute unity with that of the

Father. He ignored indeed, and refused to be bound by, the petty customs and vain traditions of men, but He most scrupulously conformed to all the requirements of the Law; was circumcised the eighth day; presented in the Temple, examined in the Law by the Jewish doctors and teachers when He was twelve years old; observed all the appointed fasts and feasts; conformed even to customs not enjoined in the Law, which were good and wise in themselves. "As His custom was He went into the synagogue on the Sabbath day." He fulfilled all the ceremonial requirements of the Law. Its offerings, oblations and sacrifices pointed to Him. Whatever other purpose they served it is certain that they witnessed to Him; to the need of a Saviour; to the need of atonement, of a Priest, a Mediator between God and man, and so to "His meritorious Cross and Passion, whereby alone we obtain remission of our sins, and are made partakers of the kingdom of heaven." He fulfilled, too, all that the Prophets had spoken concerning Him. That long line of holy men of old time, told of in the *Te Deum* as "the goodly fellowship of the Prophets," had primarily, no doubt, a mission to those of their own day, but the great underlying principle, the thread of gold that was always appearing and reappearing in their messages from God, was prophecy of a new and better day, that was to dawn on men, more light, greater knowledge, mercies, blessings, gifts, graces. In short they told, all along, of the long-promised Messiah and His reign ; of a King and of a Kingdom of God set up among men. Every reader of the gospels knows what a poor, petty meaning the scribes read into those great messages of the Prophets, and every Christian knows how completely Jesus Christ fulfilled not only the Law, but also the Prophets in all things concerning Himself, and in the establishment of the new and better covenant of the world-wide, spiritual kingdom.

But in another, a most important, and a less remembered way, He fulfilled the Law and the Prophets. The Greek word, *plerosai*, properly enough translated fulfil, means more a great deal than simply that He met every requirement of the Law and the Prophets. It means that He filled up, rounded out, perfected the Law and the Prophets.

We find, therefore, as we should expect to find, in Christianity the flower and fruit of that which appeared in Judaism only in the leaf and bud. Thus, for example, not only did Jesus Christ give in His teaching a far more adequate idea of God than had obtained among men, but in Him "God was manifest in the flesh." Thereafter men could say that in Him they had seen the Father. The religion of Israel was good for its day. It was not the best possible religion, but the best then possible. It was necessarily suited to the limitations of those that received it. To the Jew the Lord Jehovah was "the God of Israel," not the God and Father of us all. He was "a God of war," of might and power, an awful God, commonly thought of as somewhere far away above the sky, or as on the outermost rim of things, a dread being who betimes made incursions among men to help and guard, but above all to admonish and to punish them well. Jesus Christ our Lord made God known as now and here, to-day and all days, the omnipresent, immanent God; as "our Father who art in heaven," indeed and yet ever with us, by us, in us, without whose knowledge not even a sparrow falleth to the ground. He revealed God as not only "our Father" but as the God and Father of absolutely all men.

In short, He brought to light the before undreamed-of fact of the fatherhood of God and its correlative, the brotherhood of men. So, too, He brought life and immortality to light. It had always been suspected that something in us survives death. Immortality had been conjectured, desired, believed in, but such belief rested on no basis of known fact or clear explicit revelation. Jesus Christ brought immortality to light. Faith in a blessed hereafter now rests on the fact of His glorious Resurrection, and on the authority of His teaching.

In the words of Bishop Boyd Carpenter: "He came to make manifest eternal facts. The manifestation of the facts was a new revelation, but

it was not a revelation of those things which
were new in themselves." And as our Lord gave
a new and better covenant, so also He gave a
correspondingly better moral law. It is that not
to be lost sight of. To know and appreciate
what it means, will save us from all sorts of difficulties and perplexities. For one thing it reminds us that Christians are in no way responsible for Jewish morals, manners, or superstitions.
The shallow skeptic turns triumphantly to some
passage in the Old Testament that exhibits the
imperfect knowledge, inadequate morals and
manners of a rude and long-gone day, saying,
" Are we to believe that this would have place
in the record of a divine revelation ? " He might
as appropriately point to the wooden plow of
our ancestors and say, " Do you call that a
plow ? " Yes, and a very good one, too, for its
day; not the best possible, but the best then
possible. So, too, the religion of Israel was not
the ideal, the best religion, but by far the best
then possible. In fact the religion of these
Christian days is not the best possible, the ideal
religion. It will develop into something a thousand times better. The Church " without spot or
wrinkle or any such thing," will be the Church
triumphant.

But it may be well briefly to indicate how, as
our Lord gave a new and better covenant, so also
He gave a correspondingly better moral law.

The ordinary Jewish standard of righteousness

was conformity to a rigid ceremonial observance.
The Pharisee in the temple said : " I fast twice
in the week, I give tithes of all that I possess."
Jesus said, " The kingdom of God is within you,"
" From within, out of the heart of men proceed
evil thoughts," and " Woe unto you Pharisees ! for
ye tithe mint and rue and all manner of herbs, and
pass over judgment and the love of God." The
law said, " Thou shalt love thy neighbor as thy-
self," but the Jew applied it only to those of his
race and faith. Jesus said, " Ye have heard that
it hath been said thou shalt love thy neighbor
and hate thine enemy, but I say unto you, love
your enemies, bless them that curse you, do good
to them that hate you, and pray for them which
despitefully use you and persecute you ; that ye
may be the children of your Father which is in
heaven ; for He maketh His sun to rise on the
evil and on the good, and sendeth rain on the
just and on the unjust." So, too, as regards
murder, adultery, perjury, retaliation, and divorce, Jesus not only interpreted the law, but
rounded it out and filled it up by His higher
standard and teaching. The matter is admirably
summed up by Mozley in his " Ruling Ideas in
the Early Ages." " If "—he says—" there is anything in the teaching of the Old Testament that
is a falling short, which goes a certain way but
not the whole way, as in the law of marriage, in
the imperfect law of love, and in the law of retaliation, it is assumed that the essence of the

law is not all this; and that on the other hand
what is perfect is the law. We know nothing
from henceforth but the perfect law command-
ing in the conscience, 'Be ye perfect, even as
your Father who is in heaven is perfect.'

Yes, He filled up, rounded out the revelations
made aforetime. We may indeed hope for a
larger and better apprehension of His revelation
of God to men, but we cannot in this world look
for any better knowledge of God than that already revealed in Jesus Christ His Son, our Lord.

XVI.

"CHRISTUS SI NON DEUS, NON BONUS."

St. John i. 14.

XVI

"CHRISTUS, SI NON DEUS, NON BONUS."

THE Son of Man stands absolutely alone among the sons of men: not only great but incomparably the greatest of all, and yet it would hardly be reverent simply to call *Him* great, He was so vastly more than great. It is not necessary in these latter days to defend *Him*. He needs no defence. For Him at least the world now asks for no defence. Skeptics may decry Christianity, but no man—none worthy of the name—would now speak irreverently of Jesus Christ. There are indeed those ready enough to decry the Bible; reject what is called the miraculous, and bitterly assail the Christian Church, but none quite base enough to openly assail the Saviour. Even the coarse infidel orators, who revel in cheap assaults on Christianity, would hardly dare breathe a word against the Son of Man. Throughout Christendom hardly are there any so degraded as not to reverence Him. In fact, cultivated and high-minded skeptics now vie with Christians not only in proclaiming His goodness, but, practically, in acknowledging His perfection. Strauss did all he could to undermine Christianity, but was impelled to say:

"Jesus is the highest object we can possibly imagine with respect to religion. The being without whose presence in the mind perfect piety is impossible. . . . He stood alone and unapproached in history." Theodore Parker had parted altogether from "The faith once for all delivered," and yet he said: "Above all men do I bow myself before that august personage, Jesus of Nazareth. . . . He is my best historic ideal of human greatness." Carl Bahrdt was a thoroughgoing rationalist, but he said of Jesus: "O Thou great, godlike soul! no mortal can name Thy name without bending the knee, and in reverence and admiration feeling Thy unapproachable greatness! Where is the people among whom a man of this stamp has ever been born? That soul is most depraved that knows Jesus and does not love Him." Ernest Renan did his utmost to turn the gospel into a beautiful romance, and yet, however inconsistently, he bows his soul in the sacred presence of the Saviour. He says: "Christ for the first time, gave utterance to the idea upon which shall rest the edifice of the everlasting religion. He founded the pure worship —of no age—of no clime—which shall be that of all lofty souls to the end of time. . . . The words of Jesus were a gleam in a thick night; it has taken eighteen hundred years for humanity to learn to abide by it. But the gleam shall become the full day; and after passing through all the circles of error, humanity will return to these words as the immortal expression of its faith and hopes." "Repose now in Thy glory, noble Founder! Thy work is finished; Thy divinity is established. Fear no more to see the edifice of Thy labors fall by any fault. Henceforth, beyond the range of frailty, Thou shalt witness, from the heights of Divine peace, the infinite results of Thy acts. . . . Thou shalt become the corner-stone of humanity so entirely, that to tear Thy name from this world would be to rend it from its foundation. . . . Whatever may be the surprises of the future, Jesus will never be surpassed. His worship will grow young without ceasing. All ages will proclaim that, among the sons of men, there is none born greater than Jesus."

Among scholarly and high-minded historians, none stands higher than W. E. H. Lecky whose calm estimate of Christ's work is summed up in these well-known words: "It was reserved for Christianity to present to the world an ideal character, which through all the changes of eighteen centuries has inspired the hearts of men with an impassioned love, has shown itself capable of acting on all ages, nations, temperaments, and conditions; has been not only the highest pattern of virtue, but the strongest incentive to its practice; and has exercised so deep an influence that it may be truly said that the simple record of three short years of active life has done more to regenerate and soften mankind than all the disquisitions of philosophers, and all the exhortations of moralists."

It is needless, however, to summon more from the cloud of witnesses, even in the ranks of the rationalists, that gladly proclaim the incomparable supremacy of Jesus, the Christ.

All men—the exceptions are so few as not to be taken into the account—acknowledge His perfect goodness. But they do not seem to see that just because He was perfect man He was more than man; must be God and man, yet not two, but one Christ. If perfect man then He must have been what He said He was. If not, then not only was He not perfect, but so very far from being perfect that He could not be even our examplar. In truth, the logic of the well-known saying, *Christus, si non Deus, non bonus,* is simply irresistible.

He acknowledged no imperfection, fault or sin. Nay, He challenged the world to find sin in Him: "Which of you convinceth Me of sin?" He never repented. He had nothing to repent of. He said: "I am meek and lowly in heart," and yet He made more stupendous claims than mere mortal ever dreamed of in wildest flight of fancy. He claimed not only the absolute fealty of all human kind, but also the powers and prerogatives of God: "The Son of Man hath power on earth to forgive sins." Aye, more, He claimed absolute oneness with the Almighty God: "I and My Father are one;" "I came

forth from God;" "Ye are from beneath, I am
from above;" "The Father hath committed all
judgment unto the Son;" "None cometh unto
the Father but by Me;" "I am the Way, the
Truth, and the Life;" "Before Abraham was, I
AM;" "All power is given unto Me in heaven
and in earth." It is simply impossible for words
to voice more stupendous or august claims than
these of Him who nevertheless said: "Come
unto Me, all ye that labor, and are heavy laden,
and I will give you rest. Take My yoke upon
you, and learn of Me; for I am meek and lowly
of heart; and ye shall find rest unto your
souls."

Now in view of these, and the many like words
of the Lord Jesus, we must ask certain questions,
and everything pertaining to Christian believing
and living depends upon their answer: Did He
have any right to make these claims? Were
they true? Was He what He said He was?
These claims cost Him His life. They brought
Him rejection, scorn, hatred, a most cruel and
awful death. Was His Crucifixion the most
fearful crime told of in the annals of human
kind, or—for there is no other alternative—did
He, according to the law of Moses, deserve to
die? It said: "Thou shalt have no other gods
before Me;" "The prophet which shall presume
to speak a word in My name which I have not
commanded him to speak, even that prophet
shall die." He had assuredly assumed Divine

prerogatives, and on His most solemn oath before the Sanhedrim affirmed His claims. They were true or they were false.

If He was what He claimed to be, His condemnation was an unspeakable crime; but, on the other hand, if His affirmation was not true, He was guilty of blasphemy, and according to the law of Moses should have been put to death. On this ground it was that the Jews said to Pilate: "By our law He ought to die because He made Himself the Son of God."

There is no higher authority on the law of evidence than Judge Greenleaf. His calm, judicial conclusion, in reviewing the trial of Jesus, is, that on the supposition that He was a mere man, His conviction was "substantially right in point of law, though the trial was not legal in all its forms." And he adds significantly: "It is not easy to perceive on what ground His conduct could be defended before any tribunal, unless upon that of His superhuman character. No lawyer, it is conceived, would think of placing His defence on any other basis."

There is no other logical position to take. If Jesus was what He said He was, He "spake with authority," and we believe in what He said because we believe in Him. But if He was not what He claimed to be, His authoritative teaching goes for nothing, nothing at all. What He said of Himself was either true, absolutely true, or it was false and blasphemous. Therefore the inevitable inference, " *Christus, si non Deus, non bonus.*"

But He was good, absolutely good, and spake simple literal truth in saying: "Before Abraham was I am," and "He that hath seen Me hath seen the Father." "God, who at sundry times and in divers manners spake in time past unto the fathers by the prophets, hath in these last days spoken unto us by His Son." "In the beginning was the Word, and the Word was with God, and the Word was God. And the Word was made flesh, and dwelt among us, (and we beheld His glory, the glory as of the only begotten of the Father) full of grace and truth."

XVII.

"WHAT SHALL I DO THEN WITH JESUS?"

St. Matt. xxvii. 22.

XVII.

"WHAT shall I do then with Jesus which is called Christ?" It was the question of Pontius Pilate, the Roman procurator of Judea eighteen hundred years ago. He had no thought that he was asking the question of all the after ages. And yet he did. It has echoed and reëchoed in the minds of men from that day to this, and will, even unto that hour when the Son of Man shall come in the clouds of heaven, with all His holy angels, to make an end of His redemptive work, and usher in "the new heavens and the new earth wherein dwelleth righteousness." Pilate did not know it but he asked the question which you and I, and all men, must ask and answer in some way. It was meant that it should be so. At the Presentation of the Holy Child in the Temple, the aged Simeon had said to Mary, His mother, "Behold, this Child is set for the fall and rising again of many in Israel." At once the prophecy began to be fulfilled. As soon as he heard of Him Herod, the king, said what he would do with Jesus. He would kill Him. And so he "Sent forth, and slew all the children that were in Bethlehem, and in all the

125

coasts thereof." But it was not until He began
His public ministry that men generally began to
say what they would do with Jesus. He said to
one and to another, to Peter and James and
John—"Follow Me," and they followed Him:
said what they would do with Him. They
would obey Him; become His disciples; learn of
Him. Later Jesus—"Saw a man named Mat-
thew sitting at the receipt of custom: and He
saith unto him, Follow Me. And he arose and
followed Him." Still later—"A certain ruler
asked Him, saying, Good Master, what shall I
do to inherit eternal life? . . . Jesus be-
holding him loved him, and said unto him, One
thing thou lackest; go thy way, sell all that
thou hast, and give to the poor, and thou shalt
have treasure in heaven: and come, take up thy
cross, and be My disciple. And he was sad at
that saying and went away grieved; for he had
great possessions." In effect he said what he
would do with Jesus. He would not follow Him.
Nor was it to be otherwise in the still wider cir-
cle of those of that day. Whether they would or
no, everywhere, men were obliged to take sides;
obliged to say what they would do with Jesus;
obliged to be for Him or against Him. He said,
"He that is not with Me is against Me." "So
there was a division among the people concerning Him." Not only did He claim to be the
long-promised Messiah, but as such He made the
most supreme claims to the love and loyalty of

men: said, "He that loveth father or mother more than Me, is not worthy of Me;" "Before Abraham was I am;" "I and My Father are one;" "He that hath seen Me hath seen the Father;" "God so loved the world, that He gave His only-begotten Son, that whosoever believeth in Him should not perish, but have everlasting life," and "Whosoever shall confess Me before men, him will I confess before My Father which is in heaven. But whosoever shall deny Me before men, him will I deny also before My Father which is in heaven."

So it came that everywhere men were obliged to be for Him or against Him; to say what they would do with Jesus. The scribes and Pharisees, and rulers, never hesitated for a moment in saying what they would do with Him. They would kill Him. Caiaphas spake for them all in saying—"It is better for us that one man should die for the people." They decided to get rid of Him at any cost. Judas was ready to say what he would do with Him. He would betray Him for thirty pieces of silver. The members of the Sanhedrim were personally and officially obliged to say what they would do with Jesus. "They, all, condemned Him to be worthy of death." As they could not themselves pronounce sentence of death they led Him to Pilate. Having examined Him Pilate said—"I find no fault in Him." "He knew that for envy they had delivered Him." Pilate did not want to do anything with

Him. He wanted to deliver Him. When he heard that Jesus was a Galilean he sent Him to Herod. "And when Herod saw Jesus he was exceeding glad." He knew what he would do with Him. He " Set Him at naught, and mocked Him, and arrayed Him in a gorgeous robe, and sent Him again to Pilate." Pilate was more anxious than ever to deliver Him. But the rulers forced him to a decision: said—"If thou let this Man go thou art not Cæsar's friend." When it came to be a question as to expediency and duty Pilate yielded. He would not jeopardize his interests at the imperial court. To be sure " He took water, and washed his hands before the multitude, saying, I am innocent of the blood of this just person." Nevertheless—"Released he Barabbas unto them; and when he had scourged Jesus he delivered Him to be crucified." At last he answered his own question; said what he would do with Jesus. " He delivered Him to be crucified." So unwittingly he made himself infamous forever. Wherever the Creed of Christendom is said or sung we witness to what Pilate did with Jesus; say He "Suffered under Pontius Pilate."

The significant thing is that not Pilate only, but Caiaphas, Annas, Herod, the Sanhedrim, the people of Jerusalem, all were obliged to say what they would do with Jesus. They, one and all, did something. Even the very malefactors that were crucified with Jesus were obliged to say what they would do with Him. One of them confessed Him and the other died cursing Him. Nor is it otherwise with us. We are all obliged to say what we will do with Jesus. In some ways, too, it must be a more momentous matter to men now than it was to the people of Jerusalem eighteen hundred years ago. Jesus prayed that the men might be forgiven who drove the cruel nails into His holy hands, "for" (He said) "they know not what they do." We know what we do. We know what Jesus has done for men. We know what the world that He came to was; how hard and cruel and hopeless life was for men. We know what He did for men, and that in so far as light and hope, progress and blessing have come to men, it is traceable to Him who said: "I am the light of the world." Unless having eyes we see not, we know what He has done and is doing for those around us. Here and there, at least, we have seen lives sweet and beautiful with the beauty of holiness. What Jesus has done for them He would do for us also if we would let Him. Upon us, as on Pilate and those around him of old in Jerusalem, lies the necessity of saying what we will do with Jesus which is called Christ. He demands acknowledgment, love, loyalty, fealty, service. He has a right to. He makes certain, clear, explicit, well-known demands; says: "Take My yoke upon you," "Follow Me," "Learn of Me," "Do this in remembrance of Me."

He demands faith, repentance, baptism, membership in His Church, and participation in its corporate life and destiny. Every one who lives in the light of His Gospel must do one of two things; must comply with the requirements of Jesus Christ or refuse so to do. He offers pardon, help, peace, blessing. In a word salvation now and here and forever: and every man must say: "What shall I do then with Jesus which is called Christ?" He says: "Behold, I stand at the door, and knock: if any man hear My voice, and open the door, I will come in to him, and will sup with him, and he with Me." Will you let Him in, or keep Him out? Will you receive Him, or reject Him? Will you obey Him, or disobey Him; follow Him, or go your own way, "Without God, and without Christ, in the world"? He says: "My sheep hear My voice, and I know them, and they follow Me: and I give unto them eternal life; and they shall never perish, neither shall any pluck them out of My hand."

XVIII.

THE HOLY SCRIPTURES.

2 TIM. iii. 15.

XVIII.

THE name given to the Holy Scriptures is very significant. It is a significancy somewhat obscured, however, by the Greek word Bible. It would have been better if, instead of being called the Bible, these Holy Scriptures had simply been known as The Book, or The Holy Books. Such designation would better indicate their unique place.

As at our national capital there are numberless white houses, and yet only one that is called the White House, so among the countless books that have flooded the earth since the world began, one, and one only, is called The Bible—The Book. And yet this name—beautifully significant though it be—is, in a way, misleading, because the Bible is not simply a book, but a collection of books. It is to be remembered, also, that these sacred Scriptures were written by various men, at different times and widely separated stages of social development; some of them back in the very dawn of historic days others at a much later stage of civilization; that all of these Scriptures were written many centuries ago; that those of the Old Testament were written

133

long before those of the New Testament, and
that only those of the New Testament were
written in the broad daylight of historic times.

We find, then, as we should expect to find,
that these sacred Scriptures reflect the ethical,
religious, and scientific, or rather the non-scien-
tific, notions of the times in which they were
written. It need surprise no one that it should
be so. If God was to give men a revelation of
knowledge not otherwise attainable, it would, in
order to be available, necessarily be adapted to
their condition. It would be, in a sense, imperfect, and subject to limitations. In order to be
of any use to those to whom it was given, it
would, necessarily, be made in terms "under-
standed of the people"—*at the varying stages of
human development when it was given.* And yet
a remarkable characteristic of these Scriptures is
that when collected and bound up together in
one volume they make substantially one book.
Although made up of so many books, written by
so many different authors, and at such diverse
epochs and stages of civilization, the Bible is,
nevertheless, substantially one book. It is a remarkable thing that it should be so. It would
not be the case as regards any other collection
of writings in all literature. Make out, for example, a list of representative writings, from, say
the dawn of American literature to our own
times. It might begin with Cotton Mather's
"Magnalia," and end with Bryant's "Thana-

topsis." It would be seen at a glance that such a list of writings would have no coherence, no common object or purpose. And yet such a list would cover only a period of less than three hundred years. Now, recall the fact that the first of the writings that make up these sacred Scriptures was written many, many centuries before the last; that the Bible contains the most diverse kinds of literature, history, law, legend, poems, prayers, proverbs, prophecies, memoirs and letters. And yet, strange to say, this collection of writings, written so long ago, at such different times, by such different authors, at such different stages of civilization, nevertheless make one book, and the Bible as a whole is characterized by a simple organic unity. One great purpose runs through it all. It has a beginning, an ever-advancing development, and final culmination in Jesus Christ our Lord and Saviour. Then in four brief memoirs it relates the story of His life on earth; tells us of some of His many words and works, of the spread of His Church among men, and finally of the great end of His mediatorial work, the consummation of all things, the new heavens and the new earth wherein dwelleth righteousness. This unity of the sacred Scriptures is not a theory or fancy. It is a fact, and an unparalleled fact. Men talk of the possibility of a miracle. We have one here in this striking characteristic of the Scriptures. It is before our very eyes. How can we account for it? We must account for it in some way. One theory, and one only does. It is that the Bible is of God, however much it may be of men also ; that it is the record of the special revelation that He made "at sundry times and in divers manners ; " that it tells the story of His great purpose in the creation, education, redemption and salvation of humankind. If, writing to Timothy, St. Paul could speak even of the books of the Old Testament, as "The Holy Scriptures, which are able to make thee wise unto salvation through faith which is in Jesus Christ," then how much more a great deal could he have said of the Bible as a whole, " All Scripture is given by inspiration of God, and is profitable for doctrine, for reproof, for correction, for instruction in righteousness : that the man of God may be thoroughly furnished unto all good works."

XIX.

THE LIVINGNESS AND INSPIRATION OF THE SCRIPTURES.

2 TIM. iii. 16.

XIX.

THE LIVINGNESS AND INSPIRATION OF THE SCRIPTURES.

WE have seen that the various writings that make up the sacred Scriptures, though so diverse in themselves and in the time of their origination, are, nevertheless, characterized by a simple unity throughout. It is a unique fact, unparalleled in all literature.

Think of still another remarkable characteristic of the Bible; namely, its livingness and inspiration. It is the one really living book. Not one book in a million will last long. Think, for example, of the books that were popular fifty or a hundred years ago. They are for the most part forgotten now. How few now read Dryden, Pope, or even Byron. Go into any public library and ask what books are read in these days, and you will be surprised to find how modern most of them are. We should expect that it would be so as regards works on the more recent sciences. But it is largely so even in general literature. "What are the books," it was said to an eminent professor, "in your department no longer needed?" The significant answer was: "Take every book that is more than ten years old and put it in the cellar; it will be no longer needed."

The two most living books in all the world are, undoubtedly, the works of Shakespeare and the Bible. But Shakespeare is a book only of yesterday as compared with the Bible. The great dramatist died less than three hundred years ago, whereas even the last of these sacred Scriptures was written many centuries gone by, and many of the writings that make up the Old Testament were written before Athens was known or Rome was founded. Reflect upon the fact that where one man reads Shakespeare, hundreds and thousands read the Bible. Nor do they read it as they might some curious old book, but for instruction, guidance, comfort, help, hopefulness. In short, the Bible is the one great living book in all the world. Who reads the Koran, the Vedas, the Upanishads? Few indeed. And why not? Because they are dead books; books that no longer speak with living voice to living men. And why do men still read these sacred Scriptures? Why do I make the Bible my daily companion? Because it is a living book; because it inspires me. And so I *know* it to be inspired, and on the best possible evidence; namely, the fact that it is inspiring. It is not a question of belief merely, but of knowledge. I find that, by God's blessing, it feeds, nourishes, and stimulates my inner life; helps me to be a better, worthier, kinder man, than otherwise I would be.

The fact, therefore, of the inspiration of the Bible is not simply or chiefly one of learning or scholarship. It is a fact of which I am conscious. I am certain of it. To deny the fact of consciousness is to deny the groundwork not only of all belief, but of all knowledge as well. And this is the evidence—the quite sufficient evidence—for "the average man" that these Holy Scriptures are of God. It is evidence that is just as available to the poor, the unlearned, and unscientific reader, as to the scholar and the student. The inspiration of the Bible is a fact. It is not simply that it was inspired long, long ago. It inspires now, to-day, as it did aforetime.

Take, then, these Holy Scriptures and read them; take the good and holy teaching to be found in them for the guidance of your daily life, the shaping of your conduct, and you will have no great perplexities of mind as to their being indeed inspired of God the Holy Ghost. You will find that they are indeed able to make you "wise unto *salvation;*" not as to astronomy, or geology, or chemistry, but "unto salvation." As Baronius has well said, "The intention of Scripture is to tell us how to go to heaven: not to show us how the heaven goeth." Yes, now, to-day, as all along, the Bible inspires the soul that loves its good and holy teaching and tries to profit by it. Inspiration then is not only a theory but a present day fact, and any man can prove it good in his case if he really wants to do so. "If"—said our Lord—"any man will do His will "—God's will—" he shall know of the doctrine whether it be of God."

Yes, if any will do IIis will he shall know of the doctrine, and will find in the Holy Scriptures, all necessary teaching, instruction, consolation, guidance, and inspiration to a better service of God and man.

XX.

WRESTING THE SCRIPTURES.

2 PETER iii. 15, 16.

XX.

WRESTING Scriptures is an old sin and a bad one. St. Peter had to warn men against it even in his day. In the solemn last words of his Epistle he, telling of the end of all this present scene of things, said, "The day of the Lord will come as a thief in the night; in the which the heavens shall pass away with a great noise, and the elements shall melt with fervent heat, the earth also and the works that are therein shall be burned up." Then he told how such belief should influence Christian conduct: said, "Seeing then that all these things shall be dissolved, what manner of persons ought ye to be in all holy conversation and godliness, looking for and hastening unto the coming of the day of God, wherein the heavens being on fire shall be dissolved, and the elements melt with fervent heat. Nevertheless we, according to His promise, look for new heavens and a new earth, wherein dwelleth righteousness."

Now it would seem that some had denied the necessity of any such strictness of life: nor that only, but that they had quoted St. Paul's words as justifying them in so thinking. And St. Paul had said "That a man is justified by faith without the deeds of the law "—the ceremonial law of the Old Dispensation. It would seem, however, that there were those who claimed that even the moral law was not of binding obligation, and that they had perversely quoted St. Paul's words in favor of their pernicious notions. And so St. Peter came to the defence of his brother apostle: said, "Account that the long-suffering of our Lord is salvation; even as our beloved brother Paul also, according to the wisdom given unto him, hath written unto you; as also in all his Epistles, speaking in them of these things; in which are some things hard to be understood, which they that are unlearned and unstable wrest, as they do also the other Scriptures, unto their own destruction."

And what is it to wrest the Scriptures? It is to put them to torture; to tear a text out of its place, and try to make it mean that which it does not mean.

It is a common sin in this day as it was in that. There has been a long and unapostolic succession of those that wrest St. Paul's words "as they do also the other Scriptures." Many a well-meaning man has been guilty of it. Thus, one of the early fathers was filled with a laudable desire to discourage the use of hair dyes: and no wonder, but he had no right to say that Christ condemned it when He said, " Thou canst not make one hair white or black." That was wresting

Scripture. Among others Tertullian was not free from it. It would seem that in his day as in our day the ladies had queer ways of dressing their hair. They gathered it up in a kind of topknot. And Tertullian did not like it. In fact, he railed against it in an undignified sort of way, and certainly had no right to say that the Lord condemned it when He said, "No man can add one cubit unto his stature." He wrested Scripture as men do still to their hurt if not "unto their own destruction."

How often have we heard men settle, to their own satisfaction, the solemn question of the everlasting future of humankind by saying, "Does not the Bible say, 'In the place where the tree falleth, there it shall be'?" As if the awful question of the future of all souls is to be summarily decided by a supposed saying of Solomon made so many centuries ago, one, too, that has no sort of reference to the matter. The so-called "religious wars" that have distracted and disgraced Christendom in time past, largely came of this sin of wresting Scripture. Every well-informed man knows of the manifold causes that contributed to the growth of the Papacy, and yet in thousands of books and sermons men have tried to make the Master Himself responsible for it because He said "Thou art Petros, and on this petra (that is this truth that thou hast confessed that I am the Messiah) I will build My Church."

In short no end of evils have come of this sin

of wresting Scripture. By tearing a text, or piece of a text, out of its place and context, men miss its meaning and pervert its teaching. It has caused no end of false doctrine, heresy and schism. How hardly can men see that, "The letter killeth, but the spirit giveth life." A small American sect that calls itself, " *The Church of God*," was founded on the supposed necessity of literally following the example of our Lord in washing the disciples' feet. And, if a man can wholly lose sight of the plain purpose of the Lord in so doing; if he can bring himself to regard that touching incident in a hard mechanical way, he can also, no doubt, suppose that only the members of his little sect make up the great Church of God.

Some years since a rich but ignorant old man in one of our Western states, tried his hand at church making. He claimed that, because the Lord said, "Except ye become converted, and become as little children, ye shall not enter the kingdom of heaven," Christians should pass their days in flying kites, driving hoops, playing marbles and the like. It seems that he actually started a sect, made up of tramps and other vagrants, who flourished for a time on the old man's money. It was the *Reductio ad absurdum* of wresting Scripture, and sect-making.

XXI.

MORAL DIFFICULTIES IN THE BIBLE.

St. Luke xii. 48.

XXI.

MORAL DIFFICULTIES IN THE BIBLE.

THE supposed moral difficulties in the Bible are those of the Old Testament Scriptures. They would hardly trouble any one who remembers that, "The defects of the Old Testament are those of the pupil, not of the teacher." Neither individuals nor communities can know more of God than their moral condition and character permit them to know, and so the knowledge of God has necessarily been conditioned by the moral experience of men. St. Paul reminds us that it was "at sundry times and in divers manners" that God "spake in time past unto the fathers." The truth imparted "at sundry times" was necessarily imparted "in divers manners," nor that only, but necessarily accommodated to the mental and moral condition of men from generation to generation. Divine truth could only be imparted to men as they were able to bear it. Forgetful of this many seem to suppose that what would be moral difficulties to us must have been to David and Solomon and those "in the old time before them." The so-called moral difficulties in the Bible exist mostly in the minds of men who forget that there has been a gradual impartation of Divine truth with evident adaptation to the times in which it was given, and to the circumstances and associations and mental capacities of those to whom it was addressed.

The thoughtful Christian is often shocked at the moral standard of Christians of other days and lands. How much more must he expect to be often shocked at the moral standard of those of Old Testament times. The Christian standard is one thing. The old Judaic standard was another and quite a different thing. The Old Dispensation was imperfect, transitory, and vastly inferior to the Christian Dispensation. It would, then, be absurd to suppose that those told of in the Old Testament Scriptures should have been moved by Christian motives. In reading the Old Testament many seem to forget that the moral standards of to-day are not those of Judaism, and that all men in Christian countries are now largely influenced by distinctively Christian teaching. The high-minded Jew of to-day is a very different man from the Jew of the days of Joshua or Jeremiah. Naturally so. His ethical standard is very much that of his own country, a Christian country. Solomon, with the morals and manners of his day, would find New York or Boston a very uncomfortable city to live in. No respectable Jew would have anything to do with him. He would be promptly arrested and sent to the penitentiary for bigamy. Thought

of it may help to some sort of appreciation of
our Christian civilization as compared with that
of Jerusalem in Solomon's day. It may help us
to see why we find, and should expect to find,
the moral standard of those told of in Old Testament history not only different in degree but in
kind from the moral standard of a Christian
people. It should help us also to some better
appreciation of what the world was then as compared with what it is now; of what our Lord
Jesus Christ has done for men. The Christian
world may be, and is, very far from conformity
to the teaching of Jesus Christ, and yet, with all
its sins and shortcomings, it is ten thousand
times better than Judea was in David's day, or
Rome was even under the rule of a Marcus
Aurelius. No sensible man will expect to find
those told of in the pages of the Old Testament re-
flecting the moral standards of Christianity. Our
morality is that of a Christian country. Theirs
was the Judaic standard of three thousand years
ago. They are to be judged by the standard of
their day, not our day. Furthermore, it is to
be remembered that Christianity is in no way
responsible for Judaic manners or morals. Our
Lord distinctly repudiated the Jewish standards
of eighteen hundred years ago: said explicitly
that He came to fulfil, fill up, supplement, the
Law and the Prophets. He said: "Ye have
heard that it was said by them of old time,
Thou shall not commit adultery: but I say unto

you, That whosoever looketh on a woman to lust after her hath committed adultery with her already in his heart. Ye have heard that it hath been said, Thou shalt love thy neighbor, and hate thine enemy. But I say unto you, Love your enemies, bless them that curse you, do good to them that hate you, and pray for them that despitefully use you and persecute you; that ye may be the children of your Father which is in heaven: for He maketh His sun to rise on the evil and the good, and sendeth rain on the just and on the unjust."

No: we are not Jews. We live in the light of Christ. We have knowledge of truth and of duty not vouchsafed to those of old time. We are to remember how our Lord said to His disciples, "Blessed are the eyes which see the things that ye see. For I tell you, that many prophets and kings have desired to see those things which ye see and have not seen them; and to hear those things which ye hear and have not heard them." And again—"That servant which knew his lord's will and prepared not himself, neither did according to his will, shall be beaten with many stripes. But he that knew not, and did commit things worthy of stripes, shall be beaten with few stripes. For unto whomsoever much is given, of him shall much be required."

XXII.

HOW TO READ THE BIBLE.

St. John v. 39.

XXII.

WE receive the Bible from the Church as the inspired Scriptures. In writing to Timothy, St. Paul speaks of them as "the sacred writings which are able to make thee wise unto salvation through faith which is in Christ Jesus," and adds, "Every Scripture inspired of God is also profitable for teaching, for reproof, for correction, for instruction which is in righteousness." As in prayer we speak to God, so in these Holy Scriptures He speaks to us. It is not the only way in which God speaks to men, but it is a particular way, and the ordinary way of our knowing His will concerning us. Hence the great importance of knowing how to read the Bible. For one thing, we should read it remembering that it is not simply one book, but made up of many books, and that in these we have an authoritative record of the special revelation of God to men. We are to remember also that it was "at sundry times in divers manners" that God "spake in time past unto the fathers by the prophets," and that these sacred Scriptures do not contain simply the record of a revelation to those of a single generation, but to those of very

157

different times and stages of mental, moral, and spiritual development. We should therefore read these Holy Scriptures with due appreciation of the relative importance of their several books. The Old Testament is a record of the special, progressive revelation that God made "in time past unto the fathers." In the nature of the case the Old Dispensation was imperfect, transitory, preparing for and leading up to that which was better.

In reading the Bible, we find, therefore—as we would expect to find—that this special revelation of God to men has necessarily been accommodated to those to whom it was given, and that, in the nature of the case, it was often adapted to those of a rude day, of childish notions, and a small and defective knowledge. We are to remember the words of the Lord Jesus, how He said, "Think not that I am come to destroy the Law or the Prophets: I am not come to destroy, but to fulfil." It is as if He had said that He came not only to accomplish "all things which were written in the law of Moses, and in the prophets, and in the Psalms," concerning Him, but to fill up, supplement, the imperfections of the earlier revelations made "unto the fathers by the prophets." We should therefore read the Old Testament Scriptures, remembering when and to whom these sacred writings were committed, and not expecting to find in them a record of the highest and best that God has done for

men ; *that* we find in Jesus Christ our Lord, and
the record of His words and works in the New
Testament Scriptures. Then, too, we should read
the Bible, remembering its relation to the Church.
The Church existed long before the Bible did.
Thus, the Old Dispensation existed from the
time of the covenant with Abraham, but further
and greater revelations were given "at sundry
times and in divers manners," and in the Old
Testament Scriptures we have the record of
them.

So, too, the Christian Church existed before
the Christian Scriptures. The Church gives us
the Bible, and in so doing tells us how we are to
interpret it in "all things which a Christian
ought to know and believe to his soul's health."
There never was a more delusive saying than
that "the Bible, and the Bible only, is the religion of Protestants." If it means anything, it
means that men are to go to the Bible and, without any other helps as to its meaning, are to find
out a faith and duty each one for himself. It is
simple enough as a theory, but it is an impracti-
cable, utterly unworkable, one. No body of
Christians in all the world would or could abide
by it. The Baptists say, "The Bible is our religion," but what they mean is, the Bible as Baptists interpret it. So, too, the Seventh-Day Bap-
tist, the Methodist, the Mennonite and all the
rest, insist that men shall interpret the Scriptures
as they do. No one of them will, so far as they

are concerned, let a man interpret the Bible for himself. They one and all insist that men shall find in the Bible what they think they find in it. The saying, "The Bible, and the Bible only," is an utter delusion. No Christian denomination has ever acted on it. On that theory no denomination could hold men together for twenty-four hours. Practically the plan of the various Christian bodies is *the Bible as we expound it.* The rule of the Romanist has been, since 1870, not "Hear the Church," but "Hear the Pope; believe what he tells you to, no matter what it may be; he is infallible, and the only man that is." It is an insuperable objection to the theory, that it has no foundation in reason or in Scripture. It is a brand-new theory. According to it no man can know twenty-four hours ahead just what he may be called upon to believe.

The position of the Anglican Communion as to "the sufficiency of the Holy Scriptures for salvation" is clearly stated in Article VI.:

Holy Scripture containeth all things necessary to salvation: so that whatsoever is not read therein, nor may be proved thereby, is not to be required of any man, that it should be believed as an article of faith, or be thought requisite or necessary to salvation. In the name of the Holy Scripture we do understand those canonical books of the Old and New Testament, of whose authority was never any doubt in the Church.

The Church has no right to add to the Faith. It is expressly said that the Faith "was once for all delivered unto the saints." The Church has no right to make conditions of salvation. They were declared for us, and once for all, by our Lord and Saviour, Jesus Christ. It is the part of the Church to keep the Faith; to transmit it pure, whole, intact, and to administer the Word and Sacraments with all fidelity to God and man. The Church has no right to go beyond the requirements recorded in Holy Scripture, but only to witness to what they are. No doubt the Bible does contain all necessary truth, but it by no means follows that every man, going only by his unaided judgment, will find out just what that truth is. It is unreasonable to think he would. It would not be so in any other matter. The law of the land is laid down in the statutes. I read them, and think them to mean this or that. The opinion of a good lawyer, however, is far better than mine. But his opinion, even, is not conclusive. The decisions of the courts hold. The decision of the Supreme Court is conclusive. As to the Christian Faith, however, we have an infallible Guide, for Jesus Christ Himself gave us the Faith when He ordained Baptism in the name of the Father, and of the Son, and of the Holy Ghost. No man, therefore, is to go to the Bible to discover a faith. Our Lord Himself gave us the Faith. We turn to the Scriptures to find it set forth, illustrated, taught, and practically applied. We are therefore to search the Scriptures in order to know their teaching and exemplify it in our conduct. In doing this the wayfaring man, though a fool in matters of mere scholarship, shall not err therein. Nay, in so doing he will, for all practical purposes, find the supposed difficulties of the Scriptures mostly imaginary. But it may be well to give a few simple rules as to how to read the Bible:

1st. Do not go to the Bible to discover a religion or formulate a faith, but to learn the practical duties of a Christian life.

2d. Read intelligently, as far as may be, understandingly, not thinking so much of the extent as of the quality of your reading. A few verses read daily, and duly considered, may be of far more profit than many chapters read in a mechanical, inconsiderate way.

3d. Read most in the most important portions of the Bible, especially in the New Testament, and, above all, of the words and works of our Lord Jesus Christ as told us in the Gospels.

4th. Read the Bible, remembering that in the Creed we have, stated in the briefest possible terms, the essential truths of Holy Scripture. It is well to remember also that the purpose of the Christian Year is to teach us these truths in a more extended way. Thus in the Creed we confess that our Lord " shall come to judge the quick and the dead." In the appointed services for the four Sundays in Advent, we hear what the Scriptures tell us as to the conditions of the final judgment. So each article of the Christian

Faith has its corresponding season in the Christian Year, and in no way can the Scriptures be read more profitably than in this immemorial method of Christian teaching. The man who believes the great verities of the Christian Faith as contained in the Apostle's Creed, and who searches the Scriptures as appointed by the Church for the several seasons of the Christian Year, will find himself well instructed in all the great doctrines of Christ, and "thoroughly furnished unto all good works."

5th. Read the Bible in the morning or early part of the day, when the mind is fresh and clear. It is the habit of many to read a chapter in the Bible just before going to bed at night, and it is a good way to end the day. Often, however, we are then too weary to read to much profit. Ten minutes passed in reading the Bible in the vigor and freshness of the morning will generally be found more profitable than half an hour devoted to such an exercise late at night, when tired out in mind and body.

6th. Read with recollection and reverence, remembering that in the Bible God speaks to us, and that we should be intent to hear.

7th. Read with prayer for enlightenment, and that you may understand what you read. In short, we should try to read the Bible thoughtfully, intelligently, reverently, and as "doers of the Word, and not hearers only." In the devotional use of God's Holy Word we can make no

better prayer than that for the second Sunday in
Advent:

Blessed Lord, who hast caused all Holy Scriptures to be written
for our learning; Grant that we may in such wise hear them, read,
mark, learn, and inwardly digest them, that by patience, and comfort of Thy holy Word, we may embrace, and ever hold fast the
blessed hope of everlasting life, which Thou hast given us in our
Saviour Jesus Christ. *Amen.*

XXIII.

FAITH AND THE FAITH.

Jude 3.

XXIII.

FAITH AND THE FAITH.

IT is a significant fact that faith was one of the few characteristics of men commended of Christ. He seemed to value it above everything else in those around Him. He praised not place or power, genius or talent, or any other of those things that men commonly care most for, but faith. And why? What is faith? Many, it is to be feared, think lightly of it because they do not know what it is. Is it capacity to believe without any reason for believing? In that case it would be the more valuable the less reason we have for it. But can any intelligent person suppose that in commending faith Christ commended credulity? If so, the "Faith Curer," who thinks that if only he teases God long enough he can be cured of a toothache, a broken bone, a dislocated joint, or any ill that flesh is heir to, and the Christian devotee who falls into raptures over the supposed relics of St. Anne, or the supposed liquefaction of the supposed blood of St. Januarius, must be blessed above others in the Israel of God. If faith means mere credulity then those poor pagans of Ephesus who worshipped "the great goddess Diana, and the image which fell down from Ju-

piter," must have had the greatest and best faith
of all, because it was not only without reason
but against reason. No, in commending faith
Christ did not commend credulity. Far from it.
He sternly discountenanced a superstitious regard for vain traditions as destructive of the
moral law, making "the commandment of God
of none effect."

Now faith was one of those great words to
which our Lord gave a wealth of meaning that
it never had before and has never since wholly
lost. Few words were oftener on His lips, and
we must have some definite idea of what He
meant by it if we would understand His teaching. But, without dwelling on theological dis-
tinctions, it will suffice to remember that the
word has two distinct meanings as used in the
New Testament.

First, and ordinarily in the teaching of our
Lord, it had reference to a certain disposition or
attitude of the soul toward God and the things
of the Spirit; toward Christ and His teaching.
In short, it indicated a state of receptivity to divine influences, and therefore to that "grace and
truth that came by Jesus Christ." And this it
was that He commended in the Roman centur-
ion, saying, "I have not found so great faith, no,
not in Israel;" and when to another He said:
"O woman, great is thy faith; be it unto thee
even as thou wilt," and again to His disciples:
"If ye have faith, and doubt not, ye shall say

unto this mountain, be thou removed, and cast
into the sea." Not that their faith would remove Olivet or other of the mountains of Pales-
tine, but that as with God all things are possible,
so to faith, which puts us in right relation to
God, all things are possible. But the word is
used in still another sense in the New Testament,
not as designating a certain disposition or attitude of the soul toward God, but as designating
a certain statement or body of revealed truth, as
when St. Paul, in going out to die a martyr's
death, said triumphantly: "I have kept the
Faith," and when St. Jude speaks of it as "The
Faith which was once for all delivered unto the
Saints." When spoken of without the definite
article, faith has reference to a personal attitude
of the soul toward God, but when spoken of as
the Faith, the word is used to designate that essential Christian doctrine, revealed by our Lord
and Saviour Jesus Christ. It is plain that in
neither the one case nor the other does the word
stand for a blind, unreasoning and unreasonable
credulity. To know and remember this will do
much toward correcting the erroneous supposition of those who seem to think that there is a
natural conflict between reason and faith. On
the contrary reason is the handmaid of religion.
It is one of God's greatest, noblest gifts. Rightly
used it leads to faith, and cannot but commend to
us the blessed truths summed up in the Faith,
even of that revelation as to God made known to

us by Jesus Christ His Son our Lord, most summarily stated in the Baptismal formulæ, and further and more fully amplified in the Creed, that one "Faith which was once for all delivered unto the saints." It "was once for all delivered unto the saints;" delivered unto them; not left to be added to as time went on by Pope or potentate or people. It rests on the revelation, and authoritative word of Jesus, the Christ, the one only infallible Teacher of men.

XXIV.

WHAT IS IT TO BE A CHRISTIAN?

Rom. viii. 29.

XXIV.

WHAT IS IT TO BE A CHRISTIAN?

CHRISTIANITY is a mighty power among men, and has been for, now, a long time; for eighteen hundred years and more. It might be supposed that all men would know what it is; what it demands: just what it is to be a Christian. And yet it does not seem to be so. The average man seems to have but a vague notion about it, and oftener than otherwise a wrong or at least inadequate thought as to what it is to be a Christian.

Some will say that all baptized people are Christians; and in a sense that is true. All baptized people are by virtue of their Baptism members of the Church Catholic, and in that sense are Christians. But no one will seriously maintain that all baptized men are practically Christians either in belief or life. Nay, among them we know may be found some of the most vicious and abandoned among men. No sane man will maintain that the fact of Baptism is any necessary evidence of godliness. What then is it to be a Christian, not in name only, but in heart and life? Some will say that those, and those only, are Christians that "have religion;"

have "experienced religion," and can tell you just when they "met with a change;" and that whatever else a man may be, without this he is not a Christian. This is the notion that obtains among the Methodists and the modern revivalists generally. It is not one, however, that can satisfy the observant and thoughtful. It is unreasonable, utterly without scriptural warrant, and contrary to observed facts. Thousands who have gone through this emotional process called "getting religion," are nevertheless living irreligiously and possibly in utter unrighteousness.

What then is it to be a Christian, a good Christian? There are those who will tell you that it consists simply in being good; that to be an upright, kind, benevolent man is to be a Christian; that it has no necessary relation to belief, Baptism, or connection with the Christian Church. This is the notion that seems to prevail among the Unitarians, and those sects generally that arrogate to themselves the name of "Liberal Christians." That this is a mistaken and utterly inadequate thought of what it is to be a Christian, hardly needs argument. There are to-day, as there always have been, many who are upright, kind, benevolent, and most worthy people, who do not accept the Christian Faith or in any way recognize Christ's authority, and, in fact have no claim whatever to the Christian name. Is there any clear certain answer to the inquiry,

"What is it to be a Christian, a good Christian?"
Yes; certainly. Christ our Lord Himself enjoined faith, repentance, Baptism, practical obedi-
ence, and these are necessary characteristics of a
Christian life. When He gave the great apostolic
commission He said: "Go ye therefore and
teach all nations, baptizing them in the name of
the Father and the Son, and of the Holy Ghost;
teaching them to observe and do all things whatsoever I have commanded you; and lo, I am with
you alway, even unto the end of the world."

There is, perhaps, no better short definition of
what it is to be a Christian than the Prayer
Book statement that "Baptism doth represent
unto us our profession; which is to follow the
example of our Saviour Christ, and to be made
like unto Him." "But how, it may be said, like
unto Him?" Certainly not like unto Him in
that wherein no one can be like unto Him. It is
to be remembered that in some respects He stood
alone, absolutely alone among men. No man
could make the claims that He made. No man
could say, "Before Abraham was I am," or "He
that hath seen Me hath seen the Father." No
man would presume to do for men what He
does. But we all can, and if really Christians,
will, be like Him in His object and purpose; in
His attitude toward God and man; will, in some
true sense, think and act toward God and man as
He did; will have that mind which was in Him,
and so "put on Christ" not in word only but in

very thought and deed. To be really a Christian then is "to be made like unto Him." This differentiates the good Christian from all other men. It is the plain, clear living line of demarcation between those who are "in Christ" and those who are not. Being a good Christian then is not to be determined by the fact of Baptism, or of privilege. It is not a matter of intellectual assent to a faith or a theology. It has no necessary connection whatever with emotional raptures or "experiences." It certainly does not consist simply in being upright, moral, and benevolent. It does consist in living relationship to the living God; in following the example of our Saviour Christ, and being "made like unto Him; that, as He died, and rose again for us, so should we, who are baptized, die from sin, and rise again unto righteousness; continually mortifying all our evil and corrupt affections, and daily proceeding in all virtue and godliness of living."

XXV.

"IF A MAN DIE SHALL HE LIVE AGAIN ?"

JOB xiv. 14.

XXV.

IF A MAN DIE SHALL HE LIVE AGAIN?"

THOUGH made so long long ago the question is as new and fresh to-day as it was in that hour when it first fell from the lips of the patriarch. It is a question which seems to have arisen in every man's mind since the world began. It may not be more frequently in the minds of men than any other question, but it certainly surpasses every other in honor, in dignity, and in its power to ennoble and sanctify human life. It may be that for the many—let us hope it is not so—the chief thing is—" What shall we eat? or, what shall we drink? or, wherewithal shall we be clothed?" and yet let us hope that there is no soul quite so dead, no heart quite so untouched of the All-Merciful, but that at some better moment at least this old, ever-recurring question will assert itself and for the time outrank every other. Though made so long ago, away back in the dawn of the world's historic day, it is still asked as eagerly as it was in those long-gone days of the patriarch. It is in truth one of those few questions that can claim absolute universality: for, turn to what land, or age, or race, you will, and it is still the same. Search what records of men you will, and in history, in philosophy, in art, in poetry, in literature, in monumental inscriptions of civilized peoples, and in the rude hieroglyphics of barbarous and of semi-barbarous tribes, you find that Job only gave voice to a query that arises in every man's mind when he said—" If a man die shall he live again ? " It is a question always asked, and, too, always answered in some way. Yes, and by a vast, an overwhelming majority in the same way, and that is in the affirmative. The exceptions have been so rare as hardly to be worth taking into the account. It has been so in the past. It is so still. Few, very few, have been willing to answer the question with a down-right negative. Even the most notorious of recent infidel orators took only an agnostic position in saying: " I say honestly, we do not know ; we cannot say ; cannot say whether death is only a dead wall or an open door ; the beginning or ending of a day ; the spreading of pinions to soar, or the folding forever of wings ; the rising or setting of a sun, or an endless life that brings light and joy to every one." Few, hardly any, have had the hardihood to answer Job's inquiry with an unqualified negative. And yet we often hear answers made in these latter days which are misleading to the unwary because while seeming to answer it in the affirmative they really do answer it in the negative. And these sophistries may well claim consideration.

And, first of all, the answer made by the ma-

terialist. "If a man die shall he live again?"
Oh yes, the materialist may say, in a sense it
can be said that he will. That is to say, his body
falls to pieces and yet it is not lost. Its mould
is broken only to be recast into some new combination. The body crumbles into dust, utterly
disappears to human sight, but only to reappear
as in the glad springtime of the year in shrub
and tree, and leaf and flower and vegetable life,
and finally in the very blood and bones of other
men, and in this sense it may be said that "if a
man die he shall live again." It is a hollow
sophistry. The immortality that he tells of is no
immortality at all: for, it is not a question as to
whether the body disappears only to reappear in
some new combination of atoms. It is whether
the man himself ceases to be; whether thought,
feeling, memory, affection, aspiration, hope and
fear, die and cease to be when once the body
dies and turns to dust again.

Our modern science tells us that no particle of
matter is ever annihilated.

It only changes from one form and combination into another. But, a question of ten thousand times more moment is whether mind, memory, affection, in a word the human soul, can
cease to be. Every one must see that in talking
about immortality, and meaning by it that the
particles of his body at death do not cease to be,
but only pass into some new combination, the
materialist is simply deceiving you by an impos-

ture in the use of terms : for, in talking about immortality we mean one thing by it, and one thing only, and that is the immortality of the soul, of the very man himself. Any other meaning put upon the word is mere jugglery. And this is a charge that may justly be brought against the anti-Christian theorists of our day. Thus, George Eliot says :

> "Oh may I join the choir invisible,
>   Of those immortal dead who live again,
>   In lives made better by their presence."

The words have a seeming devoutness, and are capable of a Christian meaning, but when we think of what she, no doubt, meant we find in them no Christian meaning at all, for, according to the creed of the Positivists, personality ceases at death ; what we call the soul is merely the result of cerebral action, and when once the brain ceases to act, thought, mind, memory, love, hope and aspiration simply collapse, are at an end forever.

And yet these Positivists will talk of God and heaven and immortality, but when you think of what these words mean to them you find that the God that they worship is Humanity, and that by immortality they do not mean the perpetuity of personality but the continuity of Humanity.

In other words the life of the parent is perpetuated in the life of his child ; one generation follows another in perpetual succession, and that that

is all the immortality there is for men. It is the
perpetuity of the race, not of the individual
member of it. It is, doubtless, in this sense that
George Eliot said :

> " Oh may I join the choir invisible,
> Of those immortal dead, who live again
> In lives made better by their presence."

There is another notable and equally deceptive
answer to the question but it is not one ever
likely to find favor in our practical, occidental
life. Its home is off in the far East where men
have time to dream away their days in subtle
fancies, and yet it has seemed to find favor with
a few. We refer to the answer of Pantheism.
It, too, says—Yes, you may say that man is immortal, but then that does not mean perpetuity
of personality. The immortality to be desired
(says the Pantheist) is reabsorption in the great
All. It says—God and the universe are one and
the same, and man is only a modification of the
great All. Everything is God—good and evil,
virtue and vice alike, and we poor beings of a
little day are but bubbles rising on the stream
of life, only ephemeral emanations from the All,
soon to be reabsorbed into the great Soul of
Things from whence we came. It is poetically
put in Sir Edwin Arnold's Light of Asia.

> " The dew is on the Lotus : Rise great sun
> And lift my leaf and mix me with the wave !
> Om Mani Padme Hum ! The sunrise comes !
> The dewdrop slips into the shining sea ! "

That is to say the "dewdrop" is the human soul. The "shining sea" is the great All of Things, and the blissful moment of final fate is when the soul, after manifold transmigrations and purgations, is at last lost in Nirvana. But the last and most common answer to that old inquiry of the patriarch is that of Agnosticism. It says: "We do not deny: neither do we affirm: we have no answer: at best it is only a great Perhaps." And so we hear it said "Why need we answer the question; why trouble ourselves about the matter? The dead, do not come back to tell what haply has befallen them. We may hope; may conjecture; may dogmatize; may formulate a creed out of our fancies or hopes or fears, but is it not better to turn our attention to matters within the range of our experiences, where certain results are attainable, than to waste time or thought or sympathy on that which after all lies in the realm of the hypothetical?" It is the most common and taking appeal of unbelief in our day. There is a seeming hard kind of sense in it. It falls in with the thoughts of the worldly. It suits the mind of the man, who, whatever else he does, means to make the most of what he can see and touch and taste. It often takes, too, with the young and strong who as yet have not passed through any great sorrow or serious disappointment, and so are still dazzled with the sight, as from their particular point of view, they look out on all the kingdoms of the world and the glory of them, and the Tempter says " All these will I give thee." But it will not be so always. When the world has betrayed them; when they know its sin and its sorrow, they will begin to see it for what it is, and say *Vanitas vanitatum!* Then, too, when separation and bereavement come, the great question will rise and clamor for an answer. Then, if not before they will say— " If a man die shall he live again ? " Yes, even now, in every better moment of our lives—and surely it is a strong argument for faith—we find it easy to believe in God and in the life of the world to come. It is only when we are at our worst, when we are down in the very dust, that dark or despairing doubts assail us, and faith is dim and our souls darkened by the shadow of a doubt as to what may be. If we think at all of the great problems of life; if we ask any questions we must ask this that is at once so old and yet so new. We must try to answer it. We know that mere science cannot herein help us. Nor can philosophy do much for us. It can only point to probabilities. It enforces the moral argument for immortality ; makes it a moral necessity.

Tennyson gave voice to the universal conviction of men in saying :

> " My own dim life should teach me this,
>   That life should live forevermore,
>   Else earth is darkness at the core,
> And dust and ashes all that is."

Yes, we can say this much at the demand of philosophy and " natural religion." They make the question a great probability that only stops short of certainty.

It has one answer and one only, that is sufficient and satisfying.

It rests on the authoritative word of the one only infallible Teacher. He tells us that we do not die. It is only the body that dies: not the soul. God is not the God of the dead but of the living. All souls live unto Him. "I am the resurrection and the life, saith the Lord: he that believeth in Me though he were dead yet shall he live: and whosoever liveth and believeth in Me shall never die." Yes, for such there is no death. There is indeed the parting of soul and body, but no interruption of livingness. All who touch the living God through the living Christ are participants already, now and here, in that indestructible eternal life over which death hath no power at all. "The gift of God is eternal life, and this life is in His Son. He that hath the Son of God hath life, and he that hath not the Son of God hath not life." If then any ask how it is with those who have gone hence in the true faith of His holy name, there comes the clear triumphant assurance—"He that believeth in Me shall never die, but is passed from death into life." It should read, "hath passed *out of death into life.*"

For every one departed this life of whom that

was true, there is light, the everlasting light of God. Poor, unknown, despised, he may have been. "Fools accounted his life madness, and his end to be without honor: how is he numbered among the children of God, and his lot is among the saints!"

Yes, "The righteous live forevermore: their reward also is with the Lord, and the care of them is with the most High. Therefore shall they receive a glorious kingdom, and a beautiful crown from the Lord's hand: for with His right hand shall He cover them, and with His arm shall He protect them." Yes, these are among the many blessed assurances. What wonder that the Psalmist said—"When I awake up after Thy likeness I shall be satisfied with it"? What wonder that the Apostle said—"It doth not yet appear what we shall be, but we know that when He shall appear we shall be like Him; for we shall see Him as He is"?

XXVI.

"WHAT WE SHALL BE."

1 John iii. 2.

XXVI.

"WHAT WE SHALL BE."

IT is a significant thing that the vast majority
of men believe, and always have believed in
the immortality of the soul. They have sought
for proof that we survive the shock of death, with
an unwearied, almost pathetic persistence. To
do so seems to be an inborn characteristic of
humankind. If a man can even imagine the conditions of the life of the world to come, he will
find multitudes ready to listen to what he has to
tell. This readily accounts for the popularity of
such books as Bickersteth's "Yesterday, To-day
and Forever," Oxenham's "Eschatology," Cham-
bers' "Life After Death," and even such books
as "The Little Pilgrim," "The Gates Ajar," and
the like. They witness to the undying interest
with which men try to make real to them the
conditions of life after death. It is this ine-
radicable desire to know how fares it with the
dead, that accounts for the fact that there has
never been any lack of those ready to accept almost any charlatanry that confidently claims to
prove that death is not the end of life. But we
cannot "prove immortality" in any such way as
we can a mathematical problem. The reasons

for faith are not mathematical but moral. And
yet the probabilities in favor of this faith far ex-
ceed those that we unhesitatingly accept in ordinary affairs. No one can prove a man's paternity
with mathematical certainty, but we may be so
sure of it that we need no proof. Moral certainty
is the legal method in the transmission of property
from father to son. The heir to a throne can
make no stronger claim but without question he
becomes king or emperor. Probability is often
so great that it may be, and often is, as unques-
tionable as a conclusion reached by a mathematical process. It is therefore sheerest folly to
belittle a moral certainty because it is not a
mathematical certainty. In the realm of the
moral and spiritual it is the only evidence possible. But man's interest in the question of his
immortality is so urgent that we need hardly
wonder that many seek for proof where in the
nature of things proof is not to be found, and often
regard this or that of vast importance in the
matter, when to us it seems to have no importance,
certainly none worthy of serious consideration.
A man comes to me with a wild light in his eyes,
saying—"Think of my Theosophy. Do you not
see how vastly important it is? It makes immortality a certainty.

I answer him: "Well, I do think of it, and I
do not see that it proves what you think it does,
and even if it did prove all that you claim, it
would not necessarily interest me. It is not

enough to 'prove immortality.' I want to know what sort of immortality it is; whether it is a desirable or undesirable immortality. If it is a desirable immortality I want to know how desirable; whether it is really worth hoping for, praying for and fighting for?"

Surely sensible men must see that it would not necessarily be a boon to "prove immortality." Immortality might not necessarily be a blessing. For one man at least it would be an everlasting curse. Infallible lips said of Judas Iscariot—"Good were it for that man if he had never been born." It is not enough to know that men go on living forever. We want to know what sort of life they are going to live. It would surely be a horrible thing to think that we are going on forever in sin, in selfishness, in strife and envy, with mean motives, petty jealousies, over-reaching, crowding and pushing, "hateful and hating one another." Surely no sane man would want the world to go on forever as it does now; would want life to go on simply for the sake of going on, with no great goal, no clear destiny, no glorious outcome of blessedness and peace, the peace of God.

To a right-minded man the heaven of the Mohammedan Prophet would be hell. All men seem anxious to know about immortality, but few seem to see the vast importance of the immortality that the Christ tells us of, or adequately appreciate what He did for the imperfect faith

that He found in men. How well has Dr.
Munger said: "When Christ entered on His
ministry of teaching He found certain doctrines
existing in Jewish theology: they were either
imperfect or germinal truths. He found a doctrine of God, partial in conception; he perfected
it by revealing the Divine fatherhood. He
found a doctrine of sin and righteousness, turning
on external conduct; He transferred it to the
heart and the spirit. He found a doctrine of reward and punishment, the main feature of which
was a place in the under and upper worlds where
pleasure was imparted and pain inflicted; He
transferred it to the soul, and made the pleasure
and the pain to proceed from within the man,
and to depend upon his character. He found
a doctrine of immortality held as mere future existence; He transformed the doctrine, even if He
did not supplant it, by calling it *life*, and con-
necting it with character. He accepts immortality, but He adds to it character. He puts in
abeyance the element of time, continuance, and
substitutes quality or character as its main feature."

With this in mind remember the words of the
Lord Jesus how He said—"This is eternal life,
that they might know Thee, the only true God,
and Jesus Christ, whom Thou hast sent;" "In
My Father's house are many mansions: if it were
not so I would have told you. I go to prepare a
place for you. And if I go to prepare a place

for you, I will come again and receive you unto
Myself: that where I am there ye may be
also;" "Father I will that they also, whom
Thou hast given Me, be with Me where I am;"
and how His disciple said: "Now are we the
sons of God, and it doth not yet appear what we
shall be; but we know that when He shall appear, we shall be like Him; for we shall see Him
as He is."